C000067732

The Adventure of the Wordy Companion

The Handy A-Z of Sherlockian Phraseology

Dr Nicko Vaughan

First edition published in 2018
© Copyright 2018 Nicko Vaughan

The right of Nicko Vaughan to be identified as the author of this work
has been asserted by her in accordance with the Copyright, Designs
and Patents Act 1998.

All rights reserved. No reproduction, copy or transmission of this
publication may be made without express prior written permission.
No paragraph of this publication may be reproduced, copied or
transmitted except with express prior written permission or in
accordance with the provisions of the Copyright Act 1956 (as
amended). Any person who commits any unauthorised act in relation
to this publication may be liable to criminal prosecution and civil
claims for damage.

Although every effort has been made to ensure the accuracy of the
information contained in this book, as of the date of publication,
nothing herein should be construed as giving advice. The opinions
expressed herein are those of the author and not of MX Publishing.

Paperback ISBN 978-1-78705-316-8
ePub ISBN 978-1-78705-317-5
PDF ISBN 978-1-78705-318-2

Published in the UK by MX Publishing
335 Princess Park Manor, Royal Drive,
London, N11 3GX
www.mxpublishing.com

Cover design by Brian Belanger.

DEDICATION

To all of my students who have loved and tolerated my obsession with Sherlock Holmes over the years. For my parents, Ruth and Tony, who can be relied upon to always pretend as though they understand what I'm writing about. For my partner, Glenn, who continues to make me cups of tea when I'm writing and never moans when I'm too busy to drink them. To Sarah Jane and her amazing eye for detail. And to every single Sherlockian around the world who is united under the banner of logic and reason.

"The world is full of obvious things which nobody by any chance ever observes." - Sherlock Holmes

Melvyn
+
Rose
Good Cone cracking!!
That for Com

INTRODUCTION

I couldn't pinpoint the exact age when I became aware of Sherlock Holmes; but I do know that, as a child, my love for the detective started with a television show rather than a book. Sitting with my grandmother on a school night watching the wonderful Jeremy Brett prance and mug his way through crime scenes, with the affable Watson by his side, became a regular occurrence. I'd have my glass of Diet Coke and bowl of snacks to the left of me and an old lady, who asked questions and talked over every scene because she never fully understood what was going on, to the right of me. And as far as I was concerned, Sherlock Holmes lived inside a small box at my Nana's bungalow, so it never occurred to me that Sherlock Holmes also lived between the pages of a book. I suppose that is something which each generation has faced since Holmes first appeared on screen. The ready-made, handsome screen idol versus your own imagination and an old-fashioned. No doubt when Barrymore and Rathbone stepped up to play the detective, there was a fear that the seduction of these walking, talking depictions of Holmes could overshadow the original literary works and, ultimately overtake them. But seeing as the first depiction of Sherlock Holmes was in Germany, in 1908 by Alwin Neuß and the books are still going strong, I don't think that fans of the written word have much to lose sleep over.

I was embarrassingly late to the literary party when it came to reading the Conan Doyle classics. I was well past my teens and into my late twenties before I read The Adventures of Sherlock Holmes. Even then, it was the result of a rough September transatlantic sea voyage rather than a wilful search for the consulting detective, which led me to the book. Our ship had run into some rather obtrusive 70-foot swells and most of the on-board entertainment had to be cancelled. This meant that our time-passing activities were restricted to sitting and staring out of a window, joining the long line of old ladies being sick over the side of the ship or reading something from the library. I bypassed the vomitus pensioners and sat in a comfy chair by a large window reading the chronicles of the world's only consulting detective, to the tinkling sounds of breaking glass in one of the neighbouring bars. As I was thrown around the grey Atlantic Ocean, spray violently hitting the window as we pitched and listed, I was cocooned within the wonderfully written stories, lost and happy in a world of Victorian crime and British society.

I was, and still am, glad that I didn't attempt to read the books as a child or as a young teenager. The language would have been inaccessible for me at the time and reading the books at that age might have put me off ever reading any more. It's a small barrier which can still cause a disconnection between the reader and the narrative, with some people never being able to get past the perceived "stuffy" nature of the work. Also, the contemporary depictions of Sherlock Holmes and Dr John Watson - created and popularised by BBC's *Sherlock* as well as the American show *Elementary*, which is broadcast on CBS - are so "present-day" that this could, in some way, make the original books feel even more removed and even less relevant to young or contemporary fiction readers.

Which is a shame, because the themes and contents of the original stories still feel current, probably because Sherlock Holmes was a character ahead of his time or, at the very least, a man drifted apart from the shackles of late 19th-century thinking. That is not to say that I am against modern interpretations of Holmes and Watson, far from it, for with each new wave comes new and exciting representations of these beloved characters and, furthermore, the creation of new fan bases which can also migrate new readers to the original stories.

That is not to say that all readers (young or old) are put off by the antiquated language of the original works. Many people, my adult self included, revel in the opportunity to become absorbed in a world of mendicants, monographs and malefactors for a few hours a day. For some, the rich and varied use of Latin, French and German phrases combined with references to musicians, painters and writers, as well as historical battles and socio-political commentary can only add to the atmosphere of these celebrated crime stories. But it is easy to see that, for others, this can become a distraction, a pause and a beat which throws them out of the story. When introducing my students to Conan Doyle's Holmes and Watson, one of the first things to come up in discussion is the use of, what they have described as, "wordy words." For those who have grown up in an environment of truncated text-speak communication and who also express themselves using emojis, the world described by a loquacious Dr John Watson can be quite the culture shock.

With my students in mind, I created a list of definitions of the wordiest "wordy words" taken from a few stories we were reading, as well as the meanings of some words, phrases and objects which are no longer in use. This grew into sourcing and translating all of the French, Latin and German phrases in the collected stories, as well as offering explanations about references to the aforementioned plays, classical musicians, battles, writers and books of which they would have little to no frame of reference. Inviting them in to understand the Victorian prose rather than circumnavigating these "wordy words" and phrases usually helps draw them further into the narrative rather than fight against it. However, no matter how many times you explain the original and innocent meaning of the word, they will always giggle at a well-placed "ejaculation" on the page. As do we all, at times.

I thought that if my band of future Sherlockians found these notes useful, then others might also find them beneficial as a guide through the language and references of the original stories. A sort of faithful companion book; a paper Watson to follow wherever the complete Holmes went, dutifully explaining and narrating part of his adventures. As well as the definitions, I've included a small extract from each story in which the words are used. This helps to give a little context, but these can also reveal a few important plot points. So, if you read the book before you've come to those points in the stories, you may find yourself staring at the business end of a 19th-century spoiler.

Having to really sit and study the Canon rather than become absorbed in the stories has been, surprisingly, pleasurable. I feel like I have a much deeper understanding of the world which Sherlock Holmes inhabits as well as a better understanding about the other characters who also live within it. I've discovered just how many words and references I've skipped over whilst reading the stories in the past, and it's certainly given me a much greater appreciation for the writing of Conan Doyle and a whole new lexicon to attempt to deploy into my everyday conversations. I spent a very long time trying to slip the *Polyphonic Motets of Lassus* into my dinner conversation and when I did, it certainly brought about a conversational *dénouement*, as Holmes might say.

Some words have continued to stick with me, "Slop-shop" being one of them. It's such a pleasing phrase to say, and it simply means a place where a person would buy cheap, and often used, ready-made clothing. I've also been told that the word is still used in parts of America to describe vintage clothing stores. The term is related to a ship's "slop-chest" as found in the sailing ships of the 18th and 19th century. These were stocked with cast-off sailors' clothing, often from sailors who deserted or died intestate, and made available for purchase by current crewmembers, who may have enlisted or been conscripted without sufficient proper clothing. You have to admit, saying, "I shall be purchasing my vesture from the city's slop-shop" is a much more colourful and interesting phrase than, "I'm buying a shirt from TK Max".

Some other words have done more than just loll about in my head trying to hijack my conversations, some have burst out and led to actual purchases. My absolute favourite newly-discovered word from the Holmes stories is the gasogene which is mentioned by Holmes in *The Adventure of the Mazarin Stone*. I loved it so much that I became obsessed with tracking one down and now I have my very own Victorian glass gasogene which sits, pride of

5

place, on the corner table of my office. As a girl I was obsessed with Soda Stream machines and so to find out that the 1800s had its very own version made me exceedingly happy. It also means that with just a simple addition of a few chemicals I, too, can charge my dull flat water with carbonic acid gas. I've not tried it yet, I'm much too scared of pressing the wrong thing and causing it to accidentally blow up.

My hope is that this reference guide is used by a number of different people in a number of different ways. From those unfamiliar with the stories of Holmes and Watson, to the younger or international *Sherlock* or *Elementary* fans who could use a helping hand with some of the British idioms or parlances and to those who are just interested in language and would like to learn a little more about a few old-fashioned words. I have also included some "wordy words" which are still used but may be unfamiliar to some readers, even though they might be used regularly by others. I would hope that everybody who reads it will discover something interesting that they didn't already know and that they try, at least once, to slip an obscure Victorian word into their everyday conversations.

A priori — translated from the Latin as "from the earlier." This refers to the idea of reasoning or having some knowledge which precedes a logical deduction rather than a conclusion brought about from observation or experience alone. Used in *The Sign of Four*, as Watson, Jones and Holmes seek out Jonathan Small and his strange partner-in-crime down amongst the men in the shipyards. "'Dirty-looking rascals, but I suppose everyone has some little immortal spark concealed about him. You would not think it, to look at them. There is no a priori probability about it. A strange enigma is man!'"

A four of gin hot — a phrase used in *A Study in Scarlet* by Constable John Rance as he recounted the events of the evening to Holmes. A four of gin hot was a drink which was regarded as having the same warming medicinal value as a hot toddy. It consisted of fourpence worth of gin with hot water and lemon. "I was a strollin' down, thinkin' between ourselves how uncommon handy a four of gin hot would be."

A soft Johnnie — here are two old English words put together to create a meaning. Soft, as in the meaning of a person being simple-minded or foolish, and a Johnnie, which was slang for a man or boy. Poor Mr. Pycroft explains his situation to Watson in *The Adventure of the Stock Broker's Clerk* but is sheepish at having, possibly, been taken in. "Of course it may work out all right, and I don't see that I could have done otherwise; but if I have lost my crib and get nothing in exchange I shall feel what a soft Johnnie I have been."

A trout in the milk — a phrase coined by Henry David Thoreau who was an American essay writer, philosopher and historian. In 1849 he wrote about the dairymen's strike, where there was a suspicion of milk being watered down. The quote refers to the fact that if a trout is found in the milk, it means the dairymen are watering down the milk using water from a stream. Holmes uses the phrase in *The Adventure of the Noble Bachelor* to explain the importance of, some, circumstantial evidence. "My whole examination served to turn my conjecture into a certainty. Circumstantial evidence is occasionally very convincing, as when you find a trout in the milk, to quote Thoreau's example."

Abbess — a woman who is in charge or at the head of an abbey of nuns. In *The Adventure of the Illustrious Client*, Holmes relays the meeting between himself, Kitty Winter and Violet de Merville. "Miss Winter's advent rather amazed her, I think, but she waved us into our respective chairs like a reverend abbess receiving two rather leprous mendicants."

Abstruse — something which is obscure or difficult to find. In *The Adventure of the Resident Patient*, Watson describes how Holmes is working on an experiment that is beyond Watson's understanding. "...we had both remained indoors all day, I because I feared with my shaken health to face the keen autumn wind while he was deep in some of those abstruse chemical investigations which absorbed him utterly as long as he was engaged upon them."

Abutted — a place with a common boundary or lying next to another place. This is how Watson described the location of the street which lay behind the shabby vista of Saxe-Coburg Square in *The Adventure of the Red-Headed League*. "It was difficult to realise as we looked at the line of fine shops and stately business premises that they really abutted on the other side upon the faded and stagnant square which we had just quitted."

Acushla — an old Irish word which is a term of affection and believed to come from the word chuisle, meaning the beating of my heart. It's a term of affection uttered by Jack McMurdo in *The Valley of Fear*, to the woman whom he adores, Ettie. Forced with the prospect of being thrown out of the boarding-house due to his association with the Freemen and finding out that his beloved is promised to another, he implores her to be his. "'Will you ruin your life and my own for the sake of this promise? Follow your heart, acushla! 'Tis a safer guide than any promise before you knew what it was that you were saying.'"

Adroit — the act of being skilful or very clever at something. In *The Disappearance of Lady Frances Carfax*, Watson congratulates himself on his fact-finding mission, yet unaware of how Holmes will react to his findings. "All this I jotted down and felt that Holmes himself could not have been more adroit in collecting his facts."

Affaire de coeur — which is translated as a matter of the heart and pertains to a love affair. It is how Holmes describes and deduces the actions and behaviours of a potential client on the pavement outside 221b Baker Street in *A Case of Identity*. "Oscillation upon the pavement always means an *affaire de coeur*. She would like advice, but is not sure that the matter is not too delicate for communication."

Ague — another term for malaria or a catch-all word for any illness which is accompanied by a high fever and shivering. Jonathan Small, in *The Sign of Four*, describes his hellish time spent in penal servitude on the Andaman Islands as he explains why he threw the Agra treasure into the Thames. "Twenty long years in that fever-ridden swamp, all day at work under the mangrove-tree, all night chained up in the filthy convict-huts, bitten by mosquitoes, racked with ague, bullied by every cursed black-faced as in Canon policeman who loved to take it out of a white man."

Almoner — an official person who delivers money or food to poor people, a common phrased used to describe a person such as this would be "a distributor of alms." When Watson finally paid a visit to Mrs. Laura Lyons at Coombe

Tracey she explained that Sir Charles Baskerville was a kind man who had helped her through her hardest times. "I knew already that Sir Charles Baskerville had made Stapleton his almoner upon several occasions, so the lady's statement bore the impress of truth upon it."

Ambuscade — this is simply an old-fashioned word for an ambush, such as the one planned by Holmes, Watson and Hopkins in *The Adventure of Black Peter*. "It was past eleven o'clock when we formed our little ambuscade. Hopkins was for leaving the door of the hut open, but Holmes was of the opinion that this would rouse the suspicions of the stranger."

Analogous — relating to an analogy, likening one thing to another. In *The Adventure of the Creeping Man*, Holmes explains to Watson his idea to write a monograph upon the use of dogs in detective work, "My line of thoughts about dogs is analogous. A dog reflects the family life. Whoever saw a frisky dog in a gloomy family, or a sad dog in a happy one?"

Antecedents — a person's ancestors or part of their family background. In *A Study in Scarlet* Gregson explains to Holmes how he caught and arrested Arthur Charpentier, whom he believed to be a wanted man, "The first difficulty which we had to contend with was the finding of this American's antecedents. Some people would have waited until their advertisements were answered, or until parties came forward and volunteered information. That is not Tobias Gregson's way of going to work." Also used in *The*

Man with the Twisted Lip, "The Lascar was known to be a man of the vilest antecedents."

Antimacassar — A piece of cloth put over the upper part of the back of a chair to protect it from dirt and hair oil. It can also be used as decoration. In *The Adventure of the Cardboard Box*, Watson notices it when describing the room and the client, Miss Cushing. "A worked antimacassar lay upon her lap and a basket of coloured silks stood upon a stool beside her."

Apocrypha — in this context it refers to examples of writing which are not considered to be genuine. Used by Holmes in *The Valley of Fear*, to describe the agony columns in the newspapers which are used as code to communicate secret messages, as in *The Adventure of the Red Circle*. Holmes explains to Watson his abilities to read cipher codes and his frustration at being sent a code he cannot, yet, break. "'Because there are many ciphers which I would read as easily as I do the apocrypha of the agony column: such crude devices amuse the intelligence without fatiguing it. But this is different.'"

Approbation — meaning to approve. In his first letter to Holmes in *The Hound of the Baskervilles*, Watson writes of the beautiful Miss Stapleton and her odd relationship with her brother from whom she is forever seeking approval when she speaks in his company. "He has certainly a very marked influence over her, for I have seen her continually glance at him as she talked as if seeking approbation for what she said. I trust that he is kind to her."

Aquiline — often used to describe Sherlock Holmes, it means "eagle-like" when describing a person who has a sharp, curved nose like an eagle's beak. This is how Watson describes the thinking Holmes in *The Man with the Twisted Lip*. "Silent, motionless, with the light shining upon his strong set aquiline features. So he sat as I dropped off to sleep..."

Ascetic — a person who has great discipline and avoids self-indulgence, commonly for reasons of religion or academic study. Here it is used to describe the countenance of the arch-enemy of Sherlock Holmes, Professor James Moriarty, in *The Final Problem*. "He is clean-shaven, pale, and ascetic-looking, retaining something of the professor in his features."

Askance — to perceive something, or someone, as suspicious or to look at it or them with a sceptical or disapproving attitude. In *The Adventure of the Red-Headed League* it is used by Watson to describe how people, unfamiliar with Sherlock Holmes' method of observation and inference, often react to his deductions. "...those who were unacquainted with his methods would look askance at him as on a man whose knowledge was not that of other mortals."

Asperity — a harsh tone filled with sharpness and one which describes the feelings of Annie Harrison in *The Adventure of the Naval Treaty* as she probes Holmes for information, "'Do you see any prospect of solving this mystery, Mr. Holmes?' she asked, with a touch of asperity in her voice. 'Oh, the *mystery!*' he answered, coming back with a start to the realities of life."

Assiduous — describes a person working industriously with a constant effort and focus on a specific task. This describes the behaviour of Reginald Musgrave's butler Brunton during the days after he has been dismissed for snooping in *The Adventure of the Musgrove Ritual*. "'For two days after, this Brunton was most assiduous in his attention to his duties. I made no allusion to what had passed, and waited with some curiosity to see how he would cover his disgrace."

Assignation — a secret rendezvous with a lover or some other clandestine appointment. In *The Adventure of The Lion's Mane*, Holmes theorises that the note found on the body of Fitzroy McPherson may indicate some kind of lover's meeting. "There was written on it in a scrawling, feminine hand: I will be there, you may be sure. — Maudie. It read like a love affair, an assignation, though when and where were a blank."

Assizes — the courts of assize, commonly known as the assizes, were courts held in the main towns of each county to hear the most serious criminal charges as well as civil cases. These were presided over by visiting judges from the higher courts based in London. Judges and their retinue of barristers, clerks, bailiffs, servants, etc. would ride a fixed series of sites to hear those cases. The term is used throughout the Canon but here we find it in *The Boscombe Valley Mystery* as the fate of suspected murder James McCarthy is relayed. "...a verdict of 'wilful murder' having been returned at the inquest on Tuesday, he was on Wednesday brought before the magistrates at Ross, who have referred the case to the next Assizes."

Astrakhan (also spelled as astrachan) — a type of dark curly lamb's fleece found in central Asia and, as Watson notes, making up part of the King of Bohemia's outfit in *A Scandal in Bohemia*. "Heavy bands of astrakhan were slashed across the sleeves and fronts of his double-breasted coat." This is also what the eponymous fiend was wearing in *The Adventure of Charles Augustus Milverton*. "A footman opened the door, and a small, stout man in a shaggy astrachan overcoat descended."

Atavism — used to describes a characteristic in a living organism that appears after being absent through many generations and/or evolutionary changes. It is heard in the conversation between Holmes and Watson in *The Adventure of the Greek Interpreter* when Holmes reveals that he has a brother, Mycroft "...at last to the question of atavism and hereditary aptitudes. The point under discussion was, how far any singular gift in an individual was due to his ancestry and how far to his own early training."

Athwart — across or from side to side, as with seats in a small boat upon which passengers or rowers sit. Used by Watson as he observes the surroundings of Mr. Thaddeus Sholto's apartment in *The Sign of Four*. "Two great tiger-skins thrown athwart it increased the suggestion of Eastern luxury, as did a huge hookah which stood upon a mat in the corner."

Avidity — to take a keen interest in something or to be enthusiastic about something. In *The Adventure of The Priory School*, Dr Watson uses the term as he observes the reaction of Sherlock Holmes to the reward money offered by the Duke of Holdernesse. "My friend rubbed his thin hands together with an appearance of avidity which was a surprise to me, who knew his frugal tastes."

Baize — A coarse wool material, usually coloured green, resembling felt and can be found covering snooker/billiard and card tables. It can also be found on the surface of a door in a residence separating the family quarters from those areas (rooms, staircases, passages, etc.) used by the servants. In the latter case, the green baize will face the residents' rooms. In part one of *The Adventure of Wisteria Lodge*, it plays its part in the cryptic note delivered to, and then discarded, by Mr. Aloysius Garcia. "Our own colours, green and white. Green open, white shut. Main stair, first corridor, seventh right, green baize. Godspeed – D."

Basaltic — refers to an igneous rock (of a lava flow) and is often seen to display a columned structure. In part two of *A Study in Scarlet* the craggy terrain and unwelcoming environment over the mountains are described to the reader when Jefferson Hope, along with John and his daughter Lucy Ferrier, escape the clutches of the Mormons in the dead of night. "On the one side a great crag towered up a thousand feet or more, black, stern, and menacing, with long basaltic columns upon its rugged surface like the ribs of some petrified monster."

Beaune — a type of wine, a red burgundy which is produced in the region around Beaune in the east of France. In *The Sign of Four*, poor Watson admonishes himself for not confronting Holmes about his frequent drug use but, after a bit of courage from his wine glass, feels he can approach the subject. "Yet upon that afternoon, whether it was the Beaune which I had taken with my lunch, or the additional exasperation produced by the extreme deliberation of his manner, I suddenly felt that I could hold out no longer."

Beeswing — potassium hydrogen tartrate or cream of tartar is a by-product of making wine. It crystallizes in wine casks during fermentation and will often form on wine corks. It creates a light, flaky substance which is often found in port and bottle-aged wines. In *The Adventure of the Abbey Grange*, Sherlock Holmes spots it in the wine glasses supposedly used by the murderers. "The three glasses were grouped together, all of them tinged with wine, and one of them containing some dregs of bees-wing. The bottle stood near them, two-thirds full, and beside it lay a long, deeply-stained cork."

Beetling — something which is projecting or standing out, a face of a rock or a person's forehead and eyebrows. The latter, along with a beard, helped with the belated identification of the escaped convict's body and not that of Sir Henry Baskerville, in *The Hound of the Baskervilles*, as Holmes and Watson turned him over on the moor. "There could be no doubt about the beetling forehead, the sunken animal eyes. It was indeed the same face which had glared

18

upon me in the light of the candle from over the rock—the face of Selden, the criminal."

Belle dame sans merci — the name of a ballad written by the poet John Keats and translated from the French as 'Beautiful woman without mercy'. The ballad offers a warning about infatuation and obsession but may also be autobiographical about Keats' illness and facing his own death. Holmes uses the phrase in *The Adventure of the Three Gables* to describe Isadora Klein and her supposed tryst with Douglas Maberle. "He was not a society butterfly but a strong, proud man who gave and expected all. But she is the 'belle dame sans merci' of fiction. When her caprice is satisfied the matter is ended."

Benares — known also as Varanasi and is a city on the banks of the Ganges. The city, which is in southeast part of Uttar Pradesh, a state located in northern India, is well known for cast sculptures, pots and utensils made out of brass and copper and decorated with intricate etchings. In *The Sign of Four*, Mary Morstan seems to be taken more by the box than the possible treasure within it. "'This is Indian work, I suppose?' 'Yes, it is Benares metal-work.' 'And so heavy!' she exclaimed, trying to raise it. 'The box alone must be of some value.'"

Bertillon system of measurements — Alphonse Bertillon was a French police officer who also worked as a biometrics researcher. He created a system of measurements of body parts and physical features, especially of the head and face, to produce a detailed description of an adult male. Women and children were excluded owing to variations in their measurements over

19

time. He also standardized the system of photographs we now know as the mug shot. The measured method of facial identification was something which Holmes enthused over, as he did with most scientific innovation, in *The Adventure of the Naval Treaty*. "His conversation, I remember, was about the Bertillon system of measurements, and he expressed his enthusiastic admiration of the French savant."

Beryl — an almost transparent pale green, blue, or yellow gemstone which is included in Watson's description of the King of Bohemia in *A Scandal in Bohemia*. His deep blue cloak was "secured at the neck with a brooch which consisted of a single flaming beryl." It is also the cause of all trouble in *The Adventure of the Beryl Coronet*. "'You have doubtless heard of the Beryl Coronet?' 'One of the most precious public possessions of the Empire,' said I."

Betimes — to be early or to make good time. In *The Adventure of the Retired Colourman*, Watson is pleased with himself for getting up early until he notices that Holmes has already breakfasted and gone out on the trail of more information. "In the morning I was up betimes, but some toast crumbs and two empty egg-shells told me that my companion was earlier still."

Billet — a position or job. Used many times within the Canon, notably in *The Adventure of the Stock Broker's Clerk* where Holmes and Watson disguise themselves as two job-seekers so they can investigate the strange goings on of Mr. Arthur Pinner. "'You are two friends of mine who are in want of a billet, and what could be more natural than that I should bring you both round to the managing director?'"

Billycock — is a style of bowler hat, a hard-felt hat with a rounded crown. It is this style of hat which is examined by Holmes in *The Adventure of the Blue Carbuncle*, whereupon he uses it to build a picture of its owner for Watson. "Its owner is unknown. I beg that you will look upon it not as a battered billycock but as an intellectual problem."

Bimetallic — Bimetallism is the term for a monetary standard where the value of money is set and defined by the value of two metals (usually gold and silver) which creates a rate of exchange between the two. The Times published an entire debate on bimetallism in 1889, in the same year 60 members of Parliament, hundreds of delegates from the Bimetallic League and a number of peers petitioned the Chancellor of the Exchequer for the government to work toward a bimetallic agreement which was international. In *The Adventure of The Bruce-Partington Plans*, this is one of the subjects which Holmes uses to explain to Watson just how his brother Mycroft is the British government. "...suppose that a minister needs information as to a point which involves the Navy, India, Canada and the bimetallic question; he could get his separate advices from various departments upon each, but only Mycroft can focus them all."

Binomial Theorem — a term used in elementary algebra which describes the expansion powers of the binomial (a polynomial that is the sum of two terms). In *The Final Problem* this is mentioned as one of the things Professor Moriarty is famed for. "At the age of twenty-one he wrote a treatise upon the Binomial Theorem, which has had a European vogue."

Blackfeet — a term written alongside the word 'Pawnees' and found in part two of *A Study in Scarlet*. "Blackfeet" refers to a Native American people or their reservation, the headquarters for the Siksikaitsitapi people located in Montana. Written as a description of the landscape of the "central portion of the great North American continent," Doyle lays out the desolate nature of the environment. "There are no inhabitants of this land of despair. A band of Pawnees or of Blackfeet may occasionally traverse it in order to reach other hunting-grounds, but the hardiest braves are glad to lose sight of those awesome plains and to find themselves once more upon their prairies." (See also Pawnees.)

Blue — a distinction which is given to those who attend Oxford or Cambridge university, it can be for representing either side in a match between the two. In *The Adventure of the Three Students*, it is used to describe one of the suspects, Gilchrist. "Gilchrist, a fine scholar and athlete; plays in the Rugby team and the cricket team for the college and got his Blue for the hurdles and the long jump."

Blue Ribbon — The 'blue-ribbon' was a badge which was worn in a buttonhole as a symbol of temperance. These badges were awarded to members of the 'Blue Ribbon Army' who pledged abstinence from alcohol. In the statement from Mr. James Browner in *The Adventure of the Cardboard Box*, he tells of the circumstances which led to him committing his most heinous crime against his wife and her male companion. "I was blue ribbon at that time, and we were putting a little money by...Then I broke my blue ribbon and began to drink again, but I think I should not have done it if Mary had been the same as ever."

Bodkin — a dagger, stiletto or a kind of thick needle. It was used during Holmes' excited explanation of his chemical discovery of a reagent which changes state with the introduction of haemoglobin and nothing else. In *A Study in Scarlet*, to test his theory that the chemical is an infallible test for blood stains, Holmes uses his own blood. "'Let's have some fresh blood,' he said, digging a long bodkin into his finger and drawing off the resulting drop of blood into a chemical pipette."

Bon vivant — translated from the French as "well living" and it refers to a person who delights in, and devotes himself to, enjoying sociable situations of good food, good drink, and good company. In *The Sign of Four*, Watson describes a more relaxed and sociable Athelney Jones during their dinner with Holmes before they set out to catch Jonathan Small and his strange partner-in-crime. "Athelney Jones proved to be a sociable soul in his hours of

23

relaxation and faced his dinner with the air of a bon vivant."

Boon — something to be thankful for like a blessing. In the second part of *The Valley of Fear*, Jack McMurdo quickly becomes the cheer of his boarding house and the talk of the town thanks to his affable personality and his quick and cheery wit. "Of an evening when they gathered together his joke was always the readiest, his conversation the brightest, and his song the best. He was a born boon companion, with a magnetism which drew good humour from all around him."

Bouguereau — William-Adolphe Bouguereau was a French painter who used themes of mythology and contemporary interpretations of classical subject matter, and one of his most notable paintings is The Birth of Venus (1879). In The Sign of Four, Mr. Thaddeus Sholto shows his sensitive and artistic side to Holmes, Watson and the delicate Mary Morstan. "I may call myself a patron of the arts. It is my weakness. The landscape is a genuine Corot, and, though a connoisseur might perhaps throw a doubt upon that Salvator Rosa, there cannot be the least question about the Bouguereau. I am partial to the modern French school."

Box — The suitcase or other storage container in which a servant transported and kept his or her clothing and other belongings. In *The Adventure of the Three Gables*, the servant Susan departs thus: "'I am clearing out of here. I've had enough of you all. I'll send for my box to-morrow.' She flounced for the door.''

Boy in buttons — is another name for a page or servant boy who is dressed in uniform and employed to run small errands for the household. There is frequent talk in 221b about getting the page to deliver messages and run tasks for Holmes. But the specific phrase "boy in buttons" is used in *A Case of Identity* to announce a client. "As he spoke there was a tap at the door, and the boy in buttons entered to announce Miss Mary Sutherland, while the lady herself loomed behind his small black figure..."

Bradshaw — George Bradshaw was a printer and publisher who created "Bradshaw's Guide," a series of train timetables and travel books which were widely used during the late 19th century. He is briefly mentioned in *The Adventure of the Copper Beeches* when Holmes needs to travel to Winchester. "'There is a train at half-past nine,' said I, glancing over my Bradshaw. 'It is due at Winchester at 11:30.'"

Brain fever — this is used frequently in the Canon and, although typically means the inflammation of the brain, the term is used in a variety of contexts. It is mostly coined, however, to suit any and all problems that were connected with the brain such as delirium, flushing, headaches, blackouts, madness and emotional shocks. In *The Adventure of the Copper Beeches*, for example, Mrs. Toller explains the dastardly plan Mr. Rucastle enacted upon his daughter. "He wanted her to sign a paper so that whether she married or not, he could use her money. When she wouldn't do it, he kept on worrying her until she got brain fever, and for six weeks was at death's door."

Brougham — a small horse-drawn carriage having four wheels and a roof which also includes an open driver's seat in the front. As he observes in *A Scandal in Bohemia*, it is this style of carriage which carries the King of Bohemia to the door of Sherlock Holmes. "A nice little brougham and a pair of beauties. A hundred and fifty guineas apiece. There's money in this case, Watson, if there is nothing else."

Brown Study — to be in a mood of deep thoughtfulness, a gloomy meditation or melancholy. The heat and quiet of Baker Street has poor Watson feeling a little moody and claustrophobic in *The Adventure of the Cardboard Box*. "I had tossed aside the barren paper, and leaning back in my chair I fell into a brown study. Suddenly my companion's voice broke in upon my thoughts."

Buckboards — a very simple, open horse-drawn carriage with a floor made of long springy boards. The seating is attached to a plank of wood between the front and rear axles. It is mentioned in *The Adventure of the Three Garridebs* in the advertisement which an excited Nathan Garrideb puts forth. "Howard Garrideb. Constructor of Agricultural Machinery Binders, reapers, steam and hand plows, drills, harrows, farmers' carts, buckboards, and all other appliances."

Bucolic — something which relates to the nice and more pleasant aspects of living in the countryside. Watson uses the word to describe the thought patterns of the local police sergeant at the Manor House of Birlstone in *The Valley of Fear*, and employs it more in the context of an insult than a mere observation. "'But, I say,' remarked the police sergeant, whose slow, bucolic common sense was still pondering the open window."

Buffs — known as the Royal East Kent Regiment, a line infantry regiment of the British Army traditionally garrisoned at Canterbury. In *The Sign of Four*, Jonathan Small begins the story of how he came to stake a claim over the Agra treasure. "I got into a mess over a girl, and could only get out of it again by taking the queen's shilling and joining the 3rd Buffs, which was just starting for India."

Bull's-eye — was a type of oil-fuelled light which was used by police officers in the 1800s. The middle part of the lamp could be moved and rotated to cut off the light from the flame and allowed officers to hide in the darkness and illuminate an object instantly. "A weary-looking police-sergeant reclined in the corner. 'Lend me your bull's-eye, sergeant,' said my companion. 'Now tie this bit of card round my neck, so as to hang it in front of me. Thank you.'" (See also Dark Lantern.)

Bulwark — a defensive wall or a person or object which acts as a defence against something. In *The Adventure of Black Peter*, on the way to the case, Watson comments on the landscape during their journey from Wayside station. "...widespread woods, which were once part of that great forest which for so long held the Saxon invaders at bay — the impenetrable 'weald,' for sixty years the bulwark of Britain."

Bumptious — a person who is irritatingly self-assertive. In *A Study in Scarlet*, Dr Watson becomes angry at, what he perceives to be, Sherlock Holmes showing off about his deductive skills, "I was still annoyed at his bumptious style of conversation. I thought it best to change the topic"

Burr — something which clings or sticks to other objects. Holmes describes how one of his Baker Street Irregulars is watching over Henry Wood, his main suspect in the murder of James Barclay in *The Adventure of the Crooked Man*. "You may be sure that I took some precautions. I have one of my Baker Street boys mounting guard over him who would stick to him like a burr, go where he might."

Calcined — to burn something until it turns to ash or calx, as was the fate of the stolen manuscript in *The Adventure of the Three Gables* by the cruel hands of Isadora Klein. "She broke into a ripple of laughter and walked to the fireplace. There was a calcined mass which she broke up with the poker. 'Shall I give this back?' she asked."

Callosities — the callus of hard skin that thickens and forms on a hand after prolonged work. An observation made by Holmes during *The Adventure of the Gloria Scott* when asked by Mr. Trevor senior to deduce him. "You have done a good deal of digging by your callosities."

Cantonments — a name for a permanent military camp or station located in India. It is where the story of Henry Wood starts in *The Adventure of the Crooked Man*, "We were in India then, in cantonments, at a place we'll call Bhurtee. Barclay, who died the other day, was sergeant in the same company as myself, and the belle of the regiment."

Canula — a piece of medical equipment which can be described as a thin tube which is inserted into a vein to administer medication (such as a drip), or to drain off fluid. It was when searching for this piece of equipment, in *The*

Adventure of the Creeping Man, that Mr. Bennett came across the mysterious carved box which belonged to Professor Presbury. "One day, in looking for a canula, I took up the box. To my surprise he was very angry, and reproved me in words which were quite savage for my curiosity."

Capricious — somebody who is given to sudden changes in mood with no obvious reason. In *The Adventure of Black Peter*, it is how Watson describes the changes in behaviour of Holmes from client to client in regards to his attitude to monetary compensation. "So unworldly was he — or so capricious — that he frequently refused his help to the powerful and wealthy where the problem made no appeal to his sympathies, while he would devote weeks of most intense application to the affairs of some humble client..."

Carbine — is a short rifle or musket which was used by cavalry and is full-length but with a short barrel. In *The Sign of Four*, Jonathan picks out this detail as he describes the convict guard who treated him badly during his incarceration. "He stood on the bank with his back to me, and his carbine on his shoulder. I looked about for a stone to beat out his brains with, but none could I see."

Carbonari — meaning "charcoal makers" which was an Italian secret society or revolution active until the 1830s. It was also a place which drew in Italian supporters who were unhappy with the repressive political climate after 1815. In *The Adventure of the Red Circle*, Gennaro Lucca, is said to have joined such a society, "My poor Gennaro, in his wild and fiery days, when all the world seemed against him and his mind was driven half mad by the injustices of life, had joined a Neapolitan society, the Red Circle, which was allied to the old Carbonari."

Carboy — with a name which derives from the Arabic word for big jug, a carboy is a large glass bottle with a short, narrow neck which is used for brewing but also for holding and storing a variety of substances, including corrosive liquids. In *The Sign of Four*, a cracked one can be found in the secret room at Pondicherry Lodge. It contained leaking creosote which hands Holmes a way to possibly trace the criminal. "You can see the outline of the edge of his small foot here at the side of this evil-smelling mess. The carboy has been cracked, you see, and the stuff has leaked out."

Catechism — a book of instructions or a series of questions which is, more often, used in reference to Christian summaries of principles. Usually this is written in a question and answer form and this is how Reginald Musgrave explains the ritual that each of the men "coming of age" within the family must go through. "He handed me the very paper which I have here, Watson, and this is the strange catechism to which each Musgrave had to submit when he came to man's estate."

Cause célèbres — a story or controversy which attracts a lot of public attention. Literally translated as "famous cases." Holmes reflects on Watson's choice of cases which he writes up and publishes in *The Adventure of the Copper*

Beeches. "You have given prominence not so much to the many causes célèbres and sensational trials in which I have figured but rather to those incidents which may have been trivial in themselves."

Cawnpore — referring to the 1857 Siege of Cawnpore which was a key episode in the Indian rebellion where an evacuation turned into a massacre. Amongst the slain were 120 British women and children who were captured and killed in the Bibighar Massacre. These murders turned the British against the Sepoy rebels and so created the battle cry, "Remember Cawnpore!" In *The Sign of Four*, Jonathan Small recalls Cawnpore as he is attacked by two Sikh troopers who were placed under his command. "If our door were in the hands of the Sepoys the place must fall, and the women and children be treated as they were in Cawnpore."

Celerity — with great speed or swiftness. After Holmes had passed on the note "shall it be the police then" to Isadora Klein in *The Adventure of the Three Gables*, it is how they are ushered inside to meet with her. "...with amazing celerity. A minute later we were in an Arabian Nights drawing-room, vast and wonderful, in a half gloom, picked out with an occasional pink electric light."

Chaffed — to be teased and mocked. The reason why the, so called, Mr. Hosmer Angel in *A Case of Identity* did not want Miss Sutherland to address letters to his office. "He said that if they were sent to the office he would be chaffed by all the other clerks about having letters from a lady."

Chaff is also used in *The Adventure of the Crooked Man*, "the smile had often been struck from his mouth, as if by some invisible hand, when he has been joining the gaieties and chaff of the mess-table."

Chagrin — the feeling of annoyance at the hands of humiliation. Used in *A Study in Scarlet* when it appears that Holmes may have been wrong about his theory regarding the pills, one of which he feeds to the sick dog. His begins to feel his reputation disintegrating in front of Watson, Gregson and Lestrade. "Holmes had taken out his watch, as minute by minute followed without result, an expression of the utmost chagrin and disappointment appeared upon his features."

Chaldean — an ancient language spoken by the inhabitants of Chaldea in 800 BC. They ruled Babylonia from 625 to 539 BC and their language is closely related to Aramaic. In *The Adventure of the Devil's Foot*, Holmes speaks of it when contemplating the Cornish language. "The ancient Cornish language had also arrested his attention, and he had, I remember, conceived the idea that it was akin to the Chaldean."

Chevy — to chase and harass something. In *The Adventure of the Naval Treaty*, Watson describes how he and his school friends would treat poor Percy Phelps. "On the contrary, it seemed rather a piquant thing to us to chevy him about the playground and hit him over the shins with a wicket."

33

Chimerical — referring to fantastical ideas and schemes. Holmes uses it in *A Study in Scarlet* when Watson appears dismissive of his article "The Book of Life" – wherein he posits that an observant man can learn all he needs from examination and inference – as a mere flight of fancy, "The theories which I have expressed there, and which you find so chimerical, are really extremely practical – so practical that I depend upon them for my bread and cheese."

Circuitous — a journey which is taken the long way (or scenic way) rather than the direct way. This is the route which Lady Carfax takes once she has departed Lausanne in *The Disappearance of Lady Frances Carfax*. "Why should not her luggage have been openly labelled for Baden? Both she and it reached the Rhenish spa by some circuitous route. This much I gathered from the manager of Cook's local office."

Circumlocution — using many words when fewer would suffice, especially during a deliberate attempt to be vague. The Duke of Holdernesse uses his directness as a chip to plead his case with Holmes in *The Adventure of the Priory School*. "You asked for frankness, Mr. Holmes, and I have taken you at your word, for I have now told you everything without an attempt at circumlocution or concealment."

Clinkers — a residue which remains after coal has burned and is commonly found in a furnace. As the out of town men descend upon the mineshaft in *The Valley of Fear*, the manager confronts them with an unfortunate, deadly consequence. "...he staggered away; but another of the assassins fired, and he went down sidewise, kicking and clawing among a heap of clinkers."

Cockaded — a cockade is a rosette or a kind of knotted ribbon worn on a hat as part of a uniform or badge of office. In *The Adventure of the Illustrious Client*, Watson describes the coachman of the client's brougham as being dressed as such which helped him, along with the coat of arms, to determine the identity of the real illustrious client. "He sprang in, gave a hurried order to the cockaded coachman, and drove swiftly away. He flung his overcoat half out of the window to cover the armorial bearings upon the panel, but I had seen them in the glare of our fanlight none the less."

Comet vintage — refers to wines where, prior to harvest, there has been a significant astrological event such as a big comet. It is also used by wine experts to describe wine which is of an exceptional quality and who believe that these astrological events help to create great wine vintages. Spoken by Watson in *The Adventure of the Stock Broker's Clerk* to describe the expression of Holmes when he is told, again, of Mr. Pycroft's mystery employer. "Then Sherlock Holmes cocked his eye at me, leaning back on the cushions with a pleased and yet critical face, like a connoisseur who has just taken his first sip of a comet vintage."

Compunction — a feeling of guilt or moral questioning which follows when a person has done something bad. This is how Watson feels as he enters into a plot to trick Irene Adler into revealing the location of the photograph in *A Scandal in Bohemia*. "I do not know whether he was seized with compunction at that moment for the part he was playing, but I know that I never felt more heartily ashamed of myself in my life than when I saw the beautiful creature against whom I was conspiring."

Commutation — a word with many different meanings but, in the context following, it means the changing of a prison sentence to something less severe. In *The Hound of the Baskervilles*, it is used in reference to the case of Selden, the Notting Hill murderer. Watson explains the reason why the courts reduced his death sentence to that of imprisonment. "The commutation of his death sentence had been due to some doubts as to his complete sanity, so atrocious was his conduct."

Condescend — to emphasise that something is beneath a person's dignity or level of importance. Used by Holmes to hurry along the pompous King of Bohemia by "lowering himself" to get on with his problem in *A Scandal in Bohemia*. "'If your Majesty would condescend to state your case,' he remarked, 'I should be better able to advise you.'"

Conflagration — a large fire which destroys a wide area of land or large amount of property. It was a fire, such as this, which reportedly killed Mr. Jonas Oldacre in *The Adventure* *of the Norwood Builder.* "The engines were soon upon the spot, but the dry wood burned with great fury, and it was impossible to arrest the conflagration until the stack had been entirely consumed."

Conic sections — a term used in geometry, when a curve is formed by the intersection of a plane with a right circular cone, yielding a circle, ellipse, or a parabola. This term was used by Holmes in *The Adventure of The Lion's Mane* when explaining the personality of math coach Ian Murdock. "He seemed to live in some high, abstract region of surds and conic sections, with little to connect him with ordinary life. He was looked upon as an oddity by the students."

Consternation — confusion or dismay resulting from a sudden amazement or feeling of dread. This is one of the reasons, as Watson tells us in *The Problem of Thor Bridge*, why some of the case notes he has from his adventures with Holmes, shall never be published. "Apart from these unfathomed cases, there are some which involve the secrets of private families to an extent which would mean consternation in many exalted quarters if it were thought possible that they might find their way into print"

Coolie — an offensive or disparaging term used at the time for unskilled labourers from Asia and India. The term is also used, with contempt, when describing a person living in Asia, India and, at times, South Africa. This term was used by Holmes as he described to Watson the cause of his terminal illness in *The Adventure of the Dying Detective*. "I know what is the matter with me. It is a coolie disease from Sumatra — a thing that the Dutch know more about than we, though they have made little of it up to date. One thing only is certain. It is infallibly deadly, and it is horribly contagious."

Copernican theory — Copernican heliocentrism was developed by mathematician and astronomer Nicolaus Copernicus and published in 1543 and placed the sun in the centre and the Earth, with the other planets, moving around it. In *A Study in Scarlet* it is one of the pieces of basic knowledge which Watson is astounded to discover that Holmes is missing. "My surprise reached a climax, however, when I found incidentally that he was ignorant of the Copernican Theory and of the composition of the Solar System."

Coping — the top of a brick or stone wall which is usually sloping or curved. This is how Watson managed to escape in the dramatic ending of The Adventure of Charles Agustus Milverton. "...I felt the hand of the man behind me grab at my ankle; but I kicked myself free and scrambled over a glass-strewn coping."

Coronet — a small and simple crown worn by lesser members of the royal family as well as peers. This is what is left by the mysterious and esteemed client as security for a £50,000 loan in *The Adventure of the Beryl Coronet*. "'You have doubtless heard of the Beryl Coronet?' 'One of the most precious public possessions of the empire,' said I.'"

Corot — is a reference to the painter Jean-Baptiste-Camille Corot who was best known as a painter of landscapes with one of his most popular works of art being

Arleux-Palluel, The Bridge of Trysts (1871 - 1872). In *The Sign of Four*, Mr. Thaddeus Sholto shows his sensitive and artistic side to Holmes, Watson and the delicate Mary Morstan. "I may call myself a patron of the arts. It is my weakness. The landscape is a genuine Corot, and, though a connoisseur might perhaps throw a doubt upon that Salvator Rosa, there cannot be the least question about the Bouguereau. I am partial to the modern French school."

Corpulent — something or somebody who is very fat or obese and the word used to describe Holmes' brother Mycroft in *The Adventure of the Greek Interpreter*. "Mycroft Holmes was a much larger and stouter man than Sherlock. His body was absolutely corpulent."

Coruscation — something which sparkles or gives off light. The flashing or sparkling of light. The term is used by Holmes during his deductions of the mystery book code which is presented to him in *The Valley of Fear*. Watson has already impressed Holmes by deducing that C2 may stand for column two and so Holmes pushes him further to find more possible answers. "Surely you do yourself an injustice. One more coruscation, my dear Watson — yet another brainwave!"

Counterpaned bed — a bed which has a quilted bedspread on top of it; the term is used to describe the bed of Miss Stoner in *The Adventure of the Speckled Band*. "A brown chest of drawers stood in one corner, a narrow white counterpaned bed in another, and a dressing-table on the left-hand side of the window."

Coup-de-maître — translates as "a master stroke" and is used by Holmes in *The Final Problem* when he talks about his nemesis Moriarty. "There are limits, you see, to our friend's intelligence. It would have been a coup-de-maître had he deduced what I would deduce and acted accordingly."

Coverlet — a type of bedspread or quilt which doesn't fit the entire bed. It was sometimes used for additional warmth, but mostly for decoration. Watson describes the shocking condition of his intimate friend, Holmes in *The Adventure of the Dying Detective*. "His eyes had the brightness of fever, there was a hectic flush upon either cheek, and dark crusts clung to his lips; the thin hands upon the coverlet twitched incessantly, his voice was croaking and spasmodic."

Creeper — this is a kind of plant which can grow on any surface and spreads itself out, growing up and along from the stem, like the creeping ivy plant. During the carriage ride in *The Hound of the Baskervilles*, Watson notes how the landscape becomes bleaker due to the wild overgrowth and the view of the stark stone cottages. "Now and then we passed a moorland cottage, walled and roofed with stone, with no creeper to break its harsh outline."

Crenelated — the crenel is a part of a building or structure which can be found on the top of castle, wall or parapet. It is the set of openings formed in the top of the structure (the solid parts are called merlons or cops) to create a "cut-out" pattern. If something is crenelated then it has these furnishings adorned upon it. In *The Hound of the Baskervilles*, Watson describes Baskerville M and the old battle towers which stand alongside it. "From this central block rose the twin towers, ancient, crenelated, and pierced with many loopholes. To right and left of the turrets were more modern wings of black granite."

Crockford — a reference to Crockford's Clerical Directory, a directory of Anglican clergymen which was named after John Crockford, a lawyer who created the book. In *The Adventure of the Retired Colourman*, Holmes uses the directory to look up J. C. Elman, the vicar of Little Purlington. "This is evidently from a responsible person, the vicar of the place. Where is my Crockford? Yes, here we have him: 'J. C. Elman, M. A., Living of Moosmoor cum Little Purlington.' Look up the trains, Watson."

Cumbrous — something which is unwieldy and difficult to manage. In *A Case of Identity*, it describes the difficult game of deception played by Mr. Windibank as he pretends to be the mysterious Mr. Angel to deceive his step-daughter. "But the deception could not be kept up forever. These pretended journeys to France were rather cumbrous. The thing to do was clearly to bring the business to an end in such a dramatic manner that it would leave a permanent impression upon the young lady's mind..."

Curare — A substance taken from the bark and stems of some South American plants and if administered to a person causes paralysis. It is traditionally used to poison arrows and blowpipe darts and it is this type of dart and poison which Holmes suspects, in *The Adventure of the Sussex Vampire*, to have caused harm to the Ferguson baby rather than its mother. "If the child were pricked with one of those arrows dipped in curare or some other devilish drug, it would mean death if the venom were not sucked out."

Curacao — this is a slightly bitter liqueur which is made from Laraha citrus peel (or the curacao orange) and was very popular in the 17th century although it is still drunk today. In *The Adventure of the Bruce Partington Plans*, Holmes offers one to Watson as he arrives to meet him at a restaurant. "Have you had something to eat? Then join me in a coffee and curacao. Try one of the proprietor's cigars. They are less poisonous than one would expect."

Cur — a cur is a name for a scruffy or aggressive mongrel dog, although it can be any kind of dog whose appearance is dirty and whose demeanour is unkempt. In the second part of *The Valley of Fear*, McGinty admires the impressive stamina and loyalty shown by Jack McMurdo after standing trial (and being acquitted). He sees him as an instrument to be used effectively in his network of crime and far superior to the other lodge members. "McGinty had instruments enough already; but he recognized that this was a supremely able one. He felt like a man holding a fierce bloodhound in leash. There were curs to do the smaller work; but someday he would slip this creature upon its prey."

Cuvier — Jean Léopold Nicolas Frédéric, Baron Cuvier, better known as George Cuvier. He was a famous French zoologist who is often described as the father of palaeontology. He is referenced by Holmes in *The Five Orange Pips* as he explains to Watson how a reasoner can deduce a chain of events from one link. "Cuvier could correctly describe a whole animal by the contemplation of a single bone, so the observer who has thoroughly understood one link in a series of incidents, should be able to accurately state all other ones..."

Cyclical dates — Chinese cyclical dates are found on Chinese porcelain. In China the cyclic calendar was popular when recording events on a short-term basis. As such Chinese porcelain can be notoriously difficult to date. In *The Adventure of the Illustrious Client*, this is one of the things which Watson learns at the request of Sherlock Holmes. "Certainly I should not like now to pose as an authority upon ceramics. And yet all that evening, and all that night with a short interval for rest, and all next morning, I was sucking in knowledge and committing names to memory. There I learned of the hall-marks of the great artist-decorators, of the mystery of cyclical dates."

Danseuse — a term for a female ballet dancer and the former occupation of Miss Flora Millar, who was arrested in connection with the vanishing of Miss Hatty Doran in *The Adventure of the Noble Bachelor*, "It appears that she was formerly a danseuse at the Allegro, and that she has known the bridegroom for some years."

Danton — Georges Danton was one of the leading forces of the French Revolution and is described by historians as the main force in the overthrowing of the French monarchy and the establishment of the First French Republic. His main rival was Maximilien Robespierre and during the Revolution Danton was seen by many as an alternative to Robespierre who wanted a new Republic based on idealistic philosophy rather than his practical approach. Robespierre also went so far as to accuse Danton and his followers of treason so he could install himself and his agents into the vacancies left within the government. In *The Valley of Fear*, McGinty mentions a county delegate who has power over several lodges and whom even the terrorising McGinty finds intimidating. "Evans Pott was his name, and even the great Boss of Vermissa felt towards him something of the repulsion and fear which the huge Danton may have felt for the puny but dangerous Robespierre."

Dark Lantern — used frequently in the stories of Holmes and Watson, this is a lantern with a sliding shutter so it can shut out the light without putting out the candle inside. In *The Adventure of the Bruce-Partington Plans*, Watson receives a note from Holmes where it is included in a list of items to bring to diner. "Am dining at Goldini's Restaurant, Gloucester Road, Kensington. Please come at once and join me there. Bring with you a jemmy, a dark lantern, a chisel, and a revolver. — S.H. It was nice equipment for a respectable citizen to carry through the dim, fog-draped streets."

Decrepitude — something which is worn out and ruined, aged or elderly. In *The Boscombe Valley Mystery* it is used to describe murder suspect Mr. John Turner "His slow, limping step and bowed shoulders gave the appearance of decrepitude, and yet his hard, deep-lined, craggy features, and his enormous limbs showed that he was possessed of unusual strength of body and of character."

Dénouement — the outcome of a situation or problem and the moment when something is finally made clear. It is also the final part of a narrative or play when all the plot strands are resolved. The word perfectly summarises how Holmes views problems as strands or links which he must neatly bring to an end. In *A Case of Identity*, Watson uses it as he rushes to 221b Baker Street to hear the conclusion of the case. "It was not until close upon six o'clock that I found myself free, and was able to spring into a hansom and drive to Baker Street, half afraid that I might be too late to assist at the dénouement of the little mystery."

De novo — starting fresh from the beginning, translated from the Latin as meaning 'from new'. As Sherlock Holmes wrenches poor Watson from the train, he can't help but think that something is not right with the case in *The Adventure of the Abbey Grange*. "Three wine-glasses, that is all. But if I had not taken things for granted, if I had examined everything with care which I would have shown had we approached the case de novo and had no cut-and-dried story to warp my mind, would I not then have found something more definite to go upon?"

De Quincey — Thomas Penson De Quincey was a writer and essayist who wrote an autobiographical work called *Confessions of an English Opium-Eater*. This is said to be the catalyst of poor Isa Whitney's opium habit at the start of *The Man with the Twisted Lip*. "The habit grew upon him, as I understand, from some foolish freak when he was at college; for having read De Quincey's description of his dreams and sensations."

Derbies — a slang word for darby cuffs, a restraint with hinges and a solid metal bar. In *The Adventure of the Red-Headed League*, they are used by Jones from Scotland Yard to restrain the cunning criminal John Clay. "He's quicker at climbing down holes than I am. Just hold out while I fix the derbies."

De Reszkes — Jean De Reszkes was a tenor singer and his brother Édouard De Reszkes was a bass. They played together in the opera *Les Huguenots* by Giacomo Meyerbeer

46

and were leading singers at the Metropolitan Opera. In *The Hound of the Baskervilles*, Holmes, after an exhaustive few cases and the tying up of the loose ends of the case at Baskerville Hall, invites Watson to relax with him at the opera. "And now, my dear Watson, we have had some weeks of severe work, and for one evening, I think, we may turn our thoughts into more pleasant channels. I have a box for 'Les Huguenots.' Have you heard the De Reszkes?"

Desultory — something which is lacking in enthusiasm and is how Watson describes the chat *en route* to the case with Mr. Alexander Holder in *The Adventure of the Beryl Coronet*. "Our client appeared to have taken fresh heart at the little glimpse of hope which had been presented to him, and he even broke into a desultory chat with me over his business affairs." Also found in *The Adventure of the Greek interpreter*. "It was after tea on a summer evening, and the conversation, which had roamed in a desultory, spasmodic fashion..."

Deuce — often heard and repeated is the phrase, "what the deuce" it can be found in many period dramas. Deuce is an old euphemism for the devil and used to express annoyance or surprise. It was certainly apt when the cry came from Count Negretto Sylvius in *The Adventure of the Mazarin Stone* when Holmes snatched the diamond from his grasp. "The Count's bewilderment overmastered his rage and fear. 'But how the deuce—?' he gasped."

Diadem — a jewelled headband or crown and another name for the coronet. It is used by Holmes as he examines it during *The Adventure of the Beryl Coronet*. "He opened the case, and taking out the diadem he laid it upon the table. It was a magnificent specimen of the jeweller's art." It can also be found in *The Adventure of the Musgrove Ritual* on the unearthing of the ancient crown of the kings of England, "There can, I think, be no doubt that this battered and shapeless diadem once encircled the brows of the royal Stuarts."

Didactic — to teach something, usually with a moral instruction and, at other times, to seem patronising. In *The Adventure of the Naval Treaty*, Holmes relays the deducting of his case to Mr. Phelps. "'The principal difficulty in your case,' remarked Holmes, in his didactic fashion, 'lay in the fact of there being too much evidence.'"

Diffidence — shy and reserved or when a person lacks confidence in his or her abilities. Such was the description of Reginald Musgrave in *The Adventure of the Musgrave Ritual*. "He was not generally popular among the undergraduates, though it always seemed to me that what was set down as pride was really an attempt to cover extreme natural diffidence." This is also how Watson starts the tale in *The Adventure of Charles Augustus Milverton*. "It is years since the incidents of which I speak took place, and yet it is with diffidence that I allude to them."

Dilettante — a person who has an interest in a subject but lacks any real commitment. In *The Adventure of the Greek*

Interpreter, this is how Holmes describes his brother Mycroft and how he uses his observation and deductive abilities. "What is to me a means of livelihood is to him the merest hobby of a dilettante."

Dio mio — literally translated from the Italian as "My God" and is cried out by Emilia Lucca in *The Adventure of the Red Circle* when she believes Holmes has killed her beloved Gennaro Lucca. "You have killed him!" she muttered. 'Oh, Dio mio, you have killed him!' Then I heard a sudden sharp intake of her breath, and she sprang into the air with a cry of joy."

Disapprobation — to disapprove or to condemn something. In his first letter to Holmes in *The Hound of the Baskervilles*, Watson writes of Sir Henry Baskerville's meeting with Miss Stapleton during their dinner at Meripit House; and the instant attraction which seemed to flourish between the two of them. An attraction which seems to irk her brother. "One would imagine that such a match would be very welcome to Stapleton, and yet I have more than once caught a look of the strongest disapprobation in his face when Sir Henry has been paying some attention to his sister."

Disconsolate — when a person is so unhappy that they are beyond being comforted. Such is the mood of the journalist Mr. Horace Harker in *The Adventure of the Six Napoleons* after he has recounted the traumatic events of that evening and attempts to write his story, "The disconsolate journalist had seated himself at a writing-table. 'I must try and make something of it,' said he, 'though I have no doubt that the first editions of the evening papers are out already with full details. It's like my luck.'"

Disjecta membra — Latin for scattered parts or fragments, usually referring to written work but in *The Adventure of the Blue Carbuncle* it is used by Mr. Henry Banks to describe what is left of his goose after it is found and eaten by Peterson, the commissionaire. "I can hardly see what use the disjecta membra of my late acquaintance are going to be to me."

Disputatious — being fond of, or taking pleasure in, having arguments. By the choice of pipe picked by Holmes, Watson is able to read his frame of mind and, in this case, knows that Holmes is eager for a 'challenging' discussion about Watson's need for the dramatic over the facts in *The Adventure of the Copper Beeches*. "...taking up a glowing cinder with the tongs and lighting with it the long cherry-wood pipe which was wont to replace his clay when he was in a disputatious rather than a meditative mood."

Dissimulation — to disguise the truth or conceal something under a false pretext. A skill which Holmes is unsure that his beloved Watson possesses nor does he rate his ability to be convincing whilst acting a lie. In *The Adventure of the Dying Detective*, after revealing his true self to Watson, Holmes remarks, "You won't be offended, Watson? You will realize that among your many talents dissimulation finds no place, and that if you had shared my secret you would never have been able to impress Smith with the urgent necessity of his presence, which was the vital point of the whole scheme."

Dissipation — an enjoyment and overindulgence in sensual pleasures. As Holmes returns from his trip to Farnham, Watson takes note of his appearance and mood in *The Adventure of the Solitary Cyclist.* "...he arrived at Baker Street late in the evening with a cut lip and a discoloured lump upon his forehead, besides a general air of dissipation which would have made his own person the fitting object of a Scotland Yard investigation."

Distrait — in a state of distraction or an absent-minded haze. It is how Holmes explains away his daydreaming incident in the carriage earlier in *Silver Blaze.* "You may remember that I was distrait, and remained sitting after you had all alighted. I was marvelling in my own mind how I could possibly have overlooked so obvious a clue." Also used in *The Adventure of the Golden Pince-Nez.* "Holmes was curiously distrait, and we walked up and down the garden path for some time in silence."

Dog-grate — this is a detachable fire grate standing in front of a fireplace upon dogs which is another name for its feet. This style of fire grate is mentioned in the first part of *The Adventure of Wisteria Lodge* where a discarded note was recovered from behind it. "It was a dog-grate, Mr. Holmes, and he over pitched it. I picked this out unburned from the back of it."

Dolichocephalic — Something which has a very long skull or a head which is longer than expected. In *The Hound of the Baskervilles*, Dr James Mortimer expresses his fascination with Holmes, his head and his brain, and so comments on his features. "You interest me very much, Mr. Holmes. I had hardly expected so dolichocephalic a skull or such well-marked supraorbital development."

Dolorously — when a person feels or expresses sorrow or distress and this is how Watson describes poor Thorneycroft Huxtable, M.A., Ph.D. in *The Adventure of the Priory School*. "The hanging pouches under the closed eyes were leaden in colour, the loose mouth drooped dolorously at the corners, the rolling chins were unshaven."

Duchess of Devonshire fashion — Georgiana Cavendish, the Duchess of Devonshire, was a socialite, style icon and fashion trendsetter. The hat Watson is commenting upon in *A Case of Identity* is, more than likely, a reference to the Gainsborough painting, Portrait of Georgiana, where she wears her ostentatious hat to the side of her head. "I saw that on the pavement opposite there stood a large woman with a heavy fur boa round her neck, and a large curling red feather in a broad-brimmed hat which was tilted in a coquettish Duchess of Devonshire fashion over her ear."

Dyspnoea — a condition whereby breathing is difficult or laboured and a catch-all term for an uncomfortable shortness of breath. In *The Hound of the Baskervilles*, Holmes is reading an article from The Devon County Chronicle which has published an account of the death of Sir Charles Baskerville and includes the state in which his body was found. "Dr Mortimer refused at first to believe that it was indeed his friend and patient who lay before him — it was explained that that is a symptom which is not unusual in cases of dyspnoea and death from cardiac exhaustion."

Écarté — translated as 'discarded,' Écarté is a two-person card game which originated in France, was very popular in the 19th century and is a little similar to the game of whist. In *The Hound of the Baskervilles*, Watson leaves Sir Henry to play a game or two with Dr Mortimer as he chats to the butler about the strange events out on the moor. "Mortimer had stayed to dinner, and he and the baronet played ecarté afterwards. The butler brought me my coffee into the library, and I took the chance to ask him a few questions."

Eddy — a small whirlpool or a current of dust or fog and used in *The Adventure of the Three Gables* to describe the keen sense for gossip held by Langdale Pike. "If ever, far down in the turbid depths of London life, there was some strange swirl or eddy, it was marked with automatic exactness by this human dial upon the surface"

Effusion — an act of talking or acting in an unrestrained or heartfelt way. This is how the first meeting of Gregson and Holmes in *A Study in Scarlet* is described, a meeting which encapsulates the enthusiasm that Gregson has for Sherlock's approval even though he is never to be convinced by the importance of "theories" over practical police work. "At the door of the house we were met by a tall, white-faced, flaxen-haired man, with a notebook in his hand, who rushed forward and wrung my companions hand with effusion."

Efficacious — when something is successful in providing its intended result and in *The Adventure of the Naval Treaty*, the result was to try and knock out poor Mr. Phelps as he took his sleeping draught. "I fancy that he had taken steps to make that draught efficacious, and that he quite relied upon your being unconscious."

Ejaculate — regardless of its modern meaning, the meaning of the word in the 1800s was shout out at something with shock or surprise. The word is peppered throughout the Canon but a few of my favourite examples are from *The Sign of Four*, "'Thank God!' I ejaculated from my very heart." *The Adventure of the Abbey Grange*, "Finally, he sprang down with an ejaculation of satisfaction." And in *The Adventure of the Naval Treaty*, Percy Phelps ejaculates three times in quick succession. "'Surely the gate was open!' ejaculated Phelps" "'The key!' ejaculated Phelps" "'Joseph!' ejaculated Phelps."

En bloc — all at once, or all at the same time, literally translated from the French as "in a block." This is the best way to tell the story of *The Adventure of the Engineer's Thumb*, according to Watson, instead of reading snippets from the newspapers. "The story has, I believe, been told more than once in the newspapers, but, like all such narratives, its effect is much less striking when set forth en bloc in a single half-column of print."

Ennui — a feeling of listlessness resulting in a lack of purpose or excitement. Used by Holmes to describe how his life feels when he is not hot upon a case and how he starts to feel at the completion of *The Adventure of the Red-Headed League*. "'It saved me from ennui,' he answered, yawning. 'Alas! I already feel it closing in upon me. My life is spent in one long effort to escape from the commonplaces of existence.'"

Enmity — the feeling of hatred or ill will with a mixture of some animosity. In part two of *A Study in Scarlet* this is used to describe the feelings of the Mormon Church and its, possibly murderous, response to the betrayal of John and his daughter Lucy Ferrier as they attempt to escape their grasp. "They had seen no signs of any pursuers, and Jefferson Hope began to think that they were fairly out of the reach of the terrible organization whose enmity they had incurred."

Entail — a law which limits inheritance over a number of generations and so keeps it within a particular family. *In The Adventure of the Priory School*, it is this law which James Wilder is keen for the Duke of Holdernesse to break. "He was eager that I should break the entail, and he was of opinion that it lay in my power to do so."

Epicurean — references a person who derives sensual joy from food and drink. In *The Adventure of the Noble Bachelor*, Watson uses the phrase to describe the food delivery which is made to Baker Street for himself, Holmes and their guests. "...to my very great astonishment, a quite epicurean little cold supper began to be laid out upon our humble lodging-house mahogany"

Epistle — a letter or series of letters. In *A Scandal in Bohemia*, it pertains to the letter left by the cunning Irene Adler for Holmes in place of the much sought-after photograph which he has been hired to retrieve. "What a woman -- oh, what a woman!' cried the King of Bohemia, when we had all three read this epistle." Also mentioned in *The Adventure of the Noble Bachelor*. "Here is a very fashionable epistle," I remarked as he entered. "Your morning letters, if I remember right, were from a fish-monger and a tide-waiter."

Epithelial — this relates to the thin tissue which forms the outer layer of a body's surface and forms part of Holmes microscopic study in *The Adventure of Shoscombe Old Place* as he examines the threads of a tweed jacket. "The irregular gray masses are dust. There are epithelial scales on the left. Those brown blobs in the centre are undoubtedly glue."

Equanimity — a calmness and composure, especially in the face of danger or difficulty. Holmes speaks to Watson in *The Final Problem* about his achievements and the impact his work has had on the criminal community. "If my record were closed tonight I could still survey it with equanimity. The air of London is the sweeter for my presence."

Erysipelas — a type of severe bacterial infection which is usually found on the face, arms or legs. In *The Adventure of the Illustrious Client*, the newspapers are told of how Holmes had contracted this infection after his stitches had been removed following a murderous attack upon him. "On the seventh day the stitches were taken out, in spite of which there was a report of erysipelas in the evening papers. The same evening papers had an announcement which I was bound, sick or well, to carry to my friend."

Execration — to damn or to denounce somebody and to put a curse upon them. When Watson meets Mr. Neil Gibson in *The Problem of Thor Bridge*, he brings to mind the terrible character assassination which Mr. Marlow Bates had delivered just moments beforehand. "As I looked upon him I understood not only the fears and dislike of his manager but also the execrations which so many business rivals have heaped upon his head."

Exhalation — an amount of fumes or vapour given off by something. In *The Adventure of the Greek Interpreter*, Watson describes the room in which Paul Kratides and Mr. Melas have been held prisoner and overcome by poisoned fumes. "From the open door there reeked a horrible poisonous exhalation which set us gasping and coughing."

Exhortation — urging a person to do something emphatically and describes Holmes' outward appearance of calm as he listens to the story of the missing Lord Saltire in *The Adventure of the Priory School*. "His drawn brows and the deep furrow between them showed that he needed no exhortation to concentrate all his attention upon a problem."

Exiguous — a small amount of something or something which, itself, is very small. As Holmes talks to inspector Alec MacDonald in *The Valley of Fear*, about his interest in Professor Moriarty, he explains his many theories about what Holmes deduces is the other, darker, side of his career. "Of course I have other reasons for thinking so — dozens of exiguous threads which lead vaguely up towards the centre of the web where the poisonous, motionless creature is lurking."

Expostulating — a strong disagreement or sense of disapproving. This is how Holmes described the clergyman in the church with Irene Alder and Godfrey Norton in *A Scandal in Bohemia*. "There was not a soul there save the two whom I had followed and a surpliced clergyman, who seemed to be expostulating with them." Also used within the works as 'expostulation'. In part two of *A Study in Scarlet*, John Ferrier is visited by a less than happy Brigham Young and must defend his position and loyalty to the Mormon Church after he has been accused of not adhering to the doctrine. "And how have I neglected it?" asked Ferrier, throwing out his hands in expostulation. "Have I not given to the common fund? Have I not attended at the Temple?"

Expound — to present something and explain its meaning. During lunch Holmes uses Watson as a sounding board for his theory in *The Boscombe Valley Mystery* . "I don't know quite what to do, and I should value your advice. Light a cigar and let me expound."

Extravasated — a word found in the study of pathology which means to force out blood from the vessels in such a way as it diffuses through the surrounding tissue. In *The Adventure of The Lion's Mane*, Holmes shows and explains to Inspector Bardle the photographs in his books of similar wounds which were found on the back of Fitzroy McPherson. "Surely it is evident that it is unequal in its intensity. There is a dot of extravasated blood here, and another there. There are similar indications in this other weal down here. What can that mean?"

Fagged — when a person is tired and exhausted. Sherlock Holmes readies himself for the arduous task of observation the next morning in *The Boscombe Valley Mystery*. "...a man should be at his very best and keenest for such nice work as that, and I did not wish to do it when fagged by a long journey."

Fait accompli — something which has already been decided upon or has already happened, forcing the outcome to be accepted. Holmes uses this in a conversation with Lord St. Simon in *The Adventure of the Noble Bachelor* whilst discussing his missing bride's dowry arrangements. "'She brought, I understand, a considerable dowry?' 'A fair dowry. Not more than is usual in my family.' 'And this, of course, remains to you, since the marriage is a fait accompli?'"

Filial — relating to a son or a daughter. In *The Adventure of the Resident Patient*, Dr Trevelyan is touched by the care his Russian patient's son shows. "I was touched by this filial anxiety. 'You would, perhaps, care to remain during the consultation?' said I."

Fifth proposition of Euclid — from the book 'The Elements' which consists of 13 essays by Euclid and puts forward the mathematical definitions and propositions under the umbrella of Euclidean geometry. The geometry of Euclid's Elements is based on five claims and of these, number five states: "If a straight line falling on two straight lines make the interior angles on the same side less than two right angles, the two straight lines, if produced indefinitely, meet on that side on which are the angles less than the two right angles." These factual and unwavering constants are used by Holmes in *The Sign of Four* to show his displeasure at Watson at straying from the science of his deductions to include a more user-friendly style of delivery. "You have attempted to tinge it with romanticism, which produces much the same effect as if you worked a love-story or an elopement into the fifth proposition of Euclid."

Florid — having a blushed or red complexion. It is used many times during *A Study in Scarlet* to describe the drunk man in the brown coat who is believed to be connected to the murder at Lauriston Gardens. "In all probability the murderer had a florid face, and the fingernails of his right hand were remarkably long." When Dr Watson enquires who will come for the false wedding ring, Holmes replies "Why, the man in the brown coat – our florid friend with the square toes"

Fog-girt — girt means to be surrounded by or closed in by. In *The Adventure of the Bruce-Partington Plans*, this is how Watson describes the room in which Holmes had previously been restlessly agitated within as he waited for a fresh problem to solve. Fog-girt is a reference to the terrible weather which was described earlier in the story. "He was a different man from the limp and lounging figure in the mouse-coloured dressing-gown who had prowled so restlessly only a few hours before round the fog-girt room,"

Foolscap — a shortened term for Foolscap folio which was the traditional paper size used in the UK and Europe before the A4 standardisation. Widely available, Foolscap writing paper would have measured 8 x 13 inches and you can find references to it in a large number of Sherlock Holmes stories. In *The Adventure of the Six Napoleons*, "As we left the room, we heard his pen travelling shrilly over the foolscap," and again in *The Hound of the Baskervilles*, "He was carefully examining the foolscap, upon which the words were pasted, holding it only an inch or two from his eyes."

Four-in-hand — this is a carriage with four horses driven by one driver and driving these carriages became a popular sport in the 1800s. So much so that a "Four-in-Hand" Driving Club was founded in 1872 when there was a revival for the sport. It is mentioned in *His Last Bow* as Von Bork and Baron Von Herling talk about the nature of the Englishman. "You yacht against them, you hunt with them, you play polo, you match them in every game, your four-in-hand takes the prize at Olympia."

Forecastle — the forward part of a ship below the deck, usually where the crew's living quarters can be found. In *The Adventure of the Cardboard Box*, James Browner talks of

Alec Fairbairn, who became a frequent visitor to his home. "...he had wonderful polite ways with him for a sailor man, so that I think there must have been a time when he knew more of the poop than the forecastle."

Forenoon — as the name suggests, something which precedes afternoon and is really just another word for late morning. In *The Adventure of the Solitary Cyclist*, this is the time of day when Miss Violet Smith rides her bike. "You must know that every Saturday forenoon I ride on my bicycle to Farnham Station in order to get the 12:22 to town."

Fowling piece — this was a firearm which was used for shooting birds or small animals. When Holmes opens the soaking wet bundle taken from the moat in *The Valley of Fear*, his attention is drawn to the significant yellow jacket contained within and its significance to the sawn-off shotgun which supposedly was used to kill Mr. Douglas. "He held it tenderly towards the light. 'Here, as you perceive, is the inner pocket prolonged into the lining in such fashion as to give ample space for the truncated fowling piece."

Fuller's-earth — a form of clay that contains a high proportion of minerals which de-colourises without chemicals. It is also very absorbent and so highly valued for absorbing oil and grease as well as being a carrier for pesticides and fertilisers. This is what Colonel Lysander Stark says his hydraulic press has been designed for in *The Adventure of the Engineer's Thumb*. "'You are probably aware that fuller's-earth is a valuable product, and that it is only found in one or two places in England?'"

Gadabout — a person who is constantly seeking pleasure. An insult thrown at Holmes by an irritated and gruff Silas Brown, owner of Mapleton Stables, in *Silver Blaze*. "I've no time to talk to every gadabout. We want no stranger here. Be off, or you may find a dog at your heels."

Garrulous — a person who talks excessively about nothing in particular, especially on trivial or unimportant matters. In *The Adventure of the Solitary Cyclist*, this is used to describe the landlord of the country pub where Holmes goes to glean information. "I was in the bar, and a garrulous landlord was giving me all that I wanted."

Gasogene — sometimes called a seltzogene, this was a Victorian device for carbonating water which looked like two balls on top of each other. The bottom sphere contained water and the top contained tartaric acid and sodium bicarbonate which would create carbon dioxide. Almost like a late Victorian Soda Stream. It was mentioned in *The Adventure of the Mazarin Stone* by Holmes as he urges Watson to make himself comfortable at 221b Baker Street once more. "But we may be comfortable in the meantime, may we not? Is alcohol permitted? The gasogene and cigars are in the old place. Let me see you once more in the customary armchair."

Gazetteer — a geographical index, not unlike a dictionary. It was used by Holmes to deduce the origin of the letter paper in *A Scandal in Bohemia*. "'...of course, stands for 'Papier.' Now for the 'Eg. Let us glance at our Continental Gazetteer.' He took down a heavy brown volume from his shelves."

Genius loci — something which was known as the protective spirit of a place; however, in a more general Western sense it means the feel of a place or the atmosphere of a location. In *The Valley of Fear*, Holmes feels he is close to solving the murder of Mr. Douglas and is convinced that a night alone in the study would help him. Watson, however, remains sceptical. "I shall sit in that room and see if its atmosphere brings me inspiration. I'm a believer in the genius loci. You smile, Friend Watson. Well, we shall see."

German Vehmgericht — the Vehmic court was a fraternal organisation from the Middle Ages who conducted vigilant style "secret" courts. They received their jurisdiction from the Holy Roman Emperor who also pronounced the capital punishments. After each execution, the bodies where usually hung from trees to warn others. In part two of *A Study in Scarlet*, John Ferrier lists it amongst historical religious extremist groups to highlight the scare tactics used by the Mormons to ensure devotion to the faith. "Not the Inquisition of Seville, nor the German Vehmgericht, nor the Secret Societies of Italy, were ever able to put a more formidable machinery in motion than that which cast a cloud over the State of Utah."

Girt — To be surrounded by or closed in by. In *The Adventure of the Bruce-Partington Plans*, this is how Watson describes the room in which Holmes had previously been restlessly agitated within as he waited for a fresh problem to solve. Fog-girt is a reference to the terrible weather which was described earlier in the story. "He was a different man from the limp and lounging figure in the mouse-coloured dressing-gown who had prowled so restlessly only a few hours before round the fog-girt room."

Goose-step — although, nowadays, the goose-step march is associated with Hitler's Nazi party, the step originated in the Prussian military. Although, the term goose-step originally referred to a British military drill where a soldier would swing one leg at a time back and forth without bending his knee. In *The Sign of Four*, Jonathan Small talks about his journey from taking the King's shilling to being part owner of a great treasure. "I wasn't destined to do much soldiering, however. I had just got past the goose-step, and learned to handle my musket, when I was fool enough to go swimming in the Ganges."

Greatcoat — a large overcoat, typically made of wool, designed as protection against very bad weather. As worn by Mr. Jabez Wilson in *The Adventure of the Red-Headed League* during his first meeting with Holmes and Watson. "The portly client puffed out his chest with an appearance of some little pride and pulled a dirty and wrinkled newspaper from the inside pocket of his greatcoat"

Grip — this is a type of case, smaller than a suitcase and was often used by travellers. This is the baggage carried by Jack McMurdo and is picked up by an awe-struck passenger travelling on the train as they make their exit after his run-in with the police in the second part of *The Valley of Fear*. "'By Gar, mate! You know how to speak to the cops,' he said in a voice of awe. 'It was grand to hear you. Let me carry your grip and show you the road.'"

Growler — a slang word for a four-wheeled, horse-drawn carriage. In the conclusion to *A Study in Scarlet*, as Holmes is revealing his deduction methods to Watson, he talks of how he managed to identify the carriage which had been at the crime scene. "I satisfied myself that it was a cab and not a private carriage by the narrow gauge of the wheels. The ordinary London growler is considerably less wide than a gentleman's brougham."

Guaiacum test — the first test used for detecting blood stains. It involved using the resin from the Guaiacum plant mixed with hydrogen peroxide to detect the presence of bloodstains by a change in colour. Holmes comments upon its unreliability in *A Study in Scarlet* in favour of his newer method. "The old guaiacum test was very clumsy and uncertain. So is the microscopic examination for blood corpuscles. The latter is valueless if the stains are a few hours old."

Gudgeon — is a small fish which is usually used by fisherman for bait to catch bigger fish but the word is also used as an insult for a stupid person who is easily fooled. This is how Holmes describes the boxer, Sam Merton, in *The Adventure of the Mazarin Stone* as opposed to the shark, Count Negretto Sylvius. "Not a bad fellow, Sam, but the Count has used him. Sam's not a shark. He is a great big silly bull-headed gudgeon. But he is flopping about in my net all the same

Harmonium — a pump organ or reed organ, the sound is made by pushing air over metal reeds from a foot bellows. One can be found in Colonel Stark's home in *The Adventure of the Engineer's Thumb*. "Colonel Stark laid down the lamp on the top of a harmonium beside the door."

Harness cask — the container used on ships for storing or soaking salt meat. An image of comparative lifestyles used by Hudson in *The Adventure of the Gloria Scott* to unnerve and threaten Mr. Trevor. "Why, it's thirty year and more since I saw you last. Here you are in your house, and me still picking my salt meat out of the harness cask."

Harried — feeling strained as a result of having demands persistently made on one; harassed; also, to ravage or to devastate, more often than not, in reference to a war or battle. Used by Watson in his first letter to Holmes in *The Hound of the Baskervilles*, he describes to Holmes the bleak and historic feel to the, as he calls it, God-forsaken corner of the world in which he is residing. He goes on to say that it is so unchanged that it feels as though the spirits of the original, bow-and-arrow-using, occupiers can still be felt all around him. "I am no antiquarian, but I could imagine that they were some unwarlike and harried race who were forced to accept that which none other would occupy."

Harum-scarum — a person who is reckless, impetuous or irresponsible. Henry Wood explains his past self to Holmes and Watson before he became the twisted wreck of a man in *The Adventure of the Crooked Man*. "I was a harum-scarum, reckless lad, and he had had an education, and was already marked for the sword-belt."

Heeled — slang word meaning armed, most likely with a gun. Abe Slaney recalls to Holmes the events of the tragic night at Ridling Thorpe Manor in *The Adventure of the Dancing Men*. "I was heeled also, and I held up my gun to scare him off and let me get away. He fired and missed me."

Henri Murger's Vie de Bohem — this is the book which Watson passes his time reading as he waits for Holmes to return from following the crooked old lady in *A Study in Scarlet*. It is an unconventional novel which follows, loosely, a number of tenuously related stories set in the Latin Quarter of Paris in the 1840s. "I had no idea how long he might be, but I sat stolidly puffing at my pipe and skipping over the pages of Henri Murger's Vie de Bohem."

Heraldic — something which relates to heraldry and how coats of arms are described. These form part of Watson's description of the gateway to Charlington Hall in *The Adventure of the Solitary Cyclist*. "There was a main gateway of lichen-studded stone, each side pillar surmounted by mouldering heraldic emblems."

Hippocratic smile — a Hippocratic face is a term sometimes used to describe the change in expression after death. Specifically, the "smile" is a term used to describe the sustained spasming of the face muscles. In *The Sign of Four*, Holmes asks Watson to place his hands on the body of unfortunate Bartholomew Sholto for his medical opinion on the man's death. "Coupled with this distortion of the face, this Hippocratic smile, or 'risus sardonicus,' as the old writers called it, what conclusion would it suggest to your mind?"

Horsham slabs — Horsham stone is a type of sandstone, high in mica and quartz, which contains the sand grains found in the Wealden clay of West Sussex. Its colour and ripple effect is said to mimic the ripples of the nearby beaches of Sussex and was a popular roofing tile. In *The Adventure of the Sussex Vampire*, Watson points out the local stone work as they arrive at the Ferguson's dwelling. "It was a large, straggling building, very old in the centre, very new at the wings with towering Tudor chimneys and a lichen-spotted, high-pitched roof of Horsham slabs."

Hottentot — was a term used in Britain (and in Europe) to describe people who were native to southwest Africa, or Khoikhoi as it was also known at the start of the 18th century. The dated term is now considered offensive and certainly should be avoided. It is used in *The Hound of the Baskervilles* by Dr Mortimer as he explains his relationship with, the now-deceased, Sir Charles Baskerville. "He had brought back much scientific information from South Africa, and many a charming evening we have spent together discussing the comparative anatomy of the Bushman and the Hottentot."

Hung-wu — was an emperor of China and founder of the Ming dynasty and so the mark of the Hung-wu would authenticate and date a piece of Ming porcelain (1368–1398). This is an area of information learned by Watson in *The Adventure of the Illustrious Client* to help Holmes catch the dreadful Baron Adelbert Gruner. "There I learned of the hall-marks of the great artist-decorators, of the mystery of cyclical dates, the marks of the Hung-wu and the beauties of the Yung-lo."

Iconoclast — a person who criticises a person's beliefs or attacks institutions and ideologies. In *The Adventure of the Six Napoleons*, Lestrade and Holmes theorise as to the motivations of the unknown smasher of Napoleon busts. "Considering how many hundreds of statues of the great Emperor must exist in London, it is too much to suppose such a coincidence as that a promiscuous iconoclast should chance to begin upon three specimens of the same bust."

Idée fixe — an obsession with something or an idea or desire which dominates the mind and actions of a person. In *The Adventure of the Six Napoleons*, Watson flexes his medical muscles for Holmes and Lestrade. "There is the condition which the modern French psychologists have called the 'Idée fixe,' which may be trifling in character, and accompanied by complete sanity in every other way."

Ignominious — to cause a public shame or to be disgraced. Holmes recounts his boxing prowess in *The Adventure of the Solitary Cyclist*. "'You are aware that I have some proficiency in the good old British sport of boxing. Occasionally it is of service. Today, for example, I should have come to very ignominious grief without it.'"

Il n'y a pas des sots si incommodes que ceux qui ont de l'esprit! — translated as 'there are no fools so inconvenient as those who have wit'. Holmes utters it as he tolerates the jibes of Mr. Athelney Jones who is another of those upholders of the law who believe in facts rather than theories. After insinuating that Holmes used mere guesswork during their last case together, Holmes is not so impressed with his deductions about the trap door at the crime scene at Pondicherry Lodge in *The Sign of Four*. "'He can find something,' remarked Holmes, shrugging his shoulders. 'He has occasional glimmerings of reason. Il n'y a pas des sots si incommodes que ceux qui ont de l'esprit!'"

Imbecility — stupidity in one's behaviour as cried by a frustrated Holmes at the failure of the police to, once again, act upon a threat to life in *The Five Orange Pips*. "Holmes shook his clenched hands in the air. "Incredible imbecility!" he cried."

Immutable — something that never changes or remains static and unable to change through time. As Watson looks around the Neolithic hut in which the strange man on the tor has been hiding out in *The Hound of the Baskervilles*, he imagines the kind of man who would be able to survive in the bleak and harsh conditions of the moors. The conclusion being that the man's mission must be of such great importance that he forces himself to endure the cold, the rain and the sparse discomfort of the historic dwelling. "When I thought of the heavy rains and looked at the gaping roof I understood how strong and immutable must be the purpose which had kept him in that inhospitable abode."

Impecunious — having very little money or having no money at all. When Holmes tells Watson of the most evil man in London, the venom cannot be held back from his speech in *The Adventure of Charles Augustus Milverton*. "This fiend has several imprudent letters, imprudent Watson, nothing worse, which were written to an impecunious young squire in the country."

Imperious — a person who is arrogant and domineering. In part two of *A Study in Scarlet*, the young Jefferson Hope realises that he has fallen deeply in love with Lucy Ferrier and so starts a complicated love tangle. "The love which had sprung up in his heart was not the sudden, changeable fancy of a boy, but rather the wild, fierce passion of a man of strong will and imperious temper."

Imperturbable — a state of calmness which cannot be upset or agitated, a person who is not easily excited. As Mr. Neil Gibson storms out of 221b Baker Street, annoyed at Holmes and his reluctance to take his case, Holmes remains his usual calm and aloof self in *The Problem of Thor Bridge*. "Our visitor made a noisy exit, but Holmes smoked in imperturbable silence with dreamy eyes fixed upon the ceiling."

Implacable — something which cannot be placated or being unable to make less angry or hostile. In *The Valley of Fear*, the past life of Mr. Douglas comes into question which may or may not have something to do with the branding mark on his arm. The idea of his having angered some secret society which sought murder as a revenge tactic, is recurring. "He imagined that some secret society, some implacable organization, was on Douglas's track, which would never rest until it killed him."

Imposture — pretending to be another person or adopting a character to fool others. In *The Adventure of the Reigate Squire*, Holmes adopts the posture and character of his "sick" self in order to divert attention as Inspector Forrester almost gives away a vital clue. "'Good heavens!' cried the Colonel, laughing, 'Do you mean to say all our sympathy was wasted and your fit an imposture?'"

Imprecations — these are offensive words or curses which are spoken or, in this case, yelled at a person. After the police burst in on Jack McMurdo after the brutal attack on the old editor, Stanger, at the Herald office in the second part of *The Valley of Fear*, he is led outside to face the jeers and insults yelled at him by the residents of the town. "Darkness had fallen, and a keen blizzard was blowing so that the streets were nearly deserted; but a few loiterers followed the group, and emboldened by invisibility shouted imprecations at the prisoner."

Inanition — exhaustion caused by having little or no nourishment. Watson comments, In *The Adventure of the Norwood Builder*, about the singular eating habits of Sherlock Holmes. "...he would permit himself no food, and I have known him to presume upon his iron strength until he has fainted from pure inanition."

Incorrigible — a person whose behaviour is unrepentant or unable to be changed. Watson uses this to describe his servant girl Mary Jane in *A Scandal in Bohemia*. "As to Mary Jane, she is incorrigible, and my wife has given her notice, but there, again, I fail to see how you work it out."

Inculpate — to accuse somebody or to blame them of something. In *The Problem of Thor Bridge*, Holmes listens to Miss Grace Dunbar's account of her meeting with Mrs. Gibson and comes to a conclusion about the gun in the wardrobe. "'That is final. Then someone came into your room and placed the pistol there in order to inculpate you.'"

Indigo-planter — indigo is a tropical plant which belongs to the pea family and the plant used to be widely cultivated as the main source of dark blue dye. Western India was the centre of the indigo cultivation and Jonathan Small, in *The Sign of Four*, explains how, after his attack by a crocodile left him invalided out, he was employed to work at one of these plantations. "A man named Abelwhite, who had come out there as an indigo-planter, wanted an overseer to look after his coolies and keep them up to their work."

Indomitable — a person's strong will or courage which cannot be overcome, a strong and unwavering bravery. When Jefferson Hope discovers the fate of his companions and his betrothed in part two of *A Study in Scarlet*, he shakes off his grief and pity and steels himself to get even with those of the Mormon Church who have wronged him. "With indomitable patience and perseverance, Jefferson Hope possessed also a power of sustained vindictiveness, which he may have learned from the Indians amongst whom he had lived."

Inestimable — something which is too large to calculate and how Watson describes how little Holmes cares about money in *The Adventure of Black Peter*. "Holmes, however, like all great artists, lived for his art's sake, and, save in the case of the Duke of Holdernesse, I have seldom known him claim any large reward for his inestimable services."

Inexorable — in this context it means a person whom it is impossible to persuade or one who is unrelenting in his outlook. Heard in a conversation about just how Mr. Hatherley was moved to safety once he passed out *in The Adventure of the Engineer's Thumb*. "'Perhaps the villain was softened by the woman's entreaties.' 'I hardly think that likely. I never saw a more inexorable face in my life.'" It is used again in *The Adventure of the Empty House* as Holmes recounts seeing Moriarty at Reichenbach Falls, "I read an inexorable purpose in his grey eyes."

Injudicious — something which is of poor judgment or an unwise thing to do or say. In *The Adventure of the Three Students*, Watson informs the reader of his decision to not go into too much detail about the location so they are unable to identify it. "It will be obvious that any details which would help the reader to exactly identify the college or the criminal would be injudicious and offensive."

Inquisition of Seville — or more widely known by Monty Python fans, as The Spanish Inquisition. The inquisition was established in 1478 and was intended to enforce Catholic orthodoxy by means of identifying heretics and executing them. In part two of *A Study in Scarlet*, John Ferrier lists it among historical religious extremist groups to highlight the scare tactics used by the Mormons to ensure devotion to the faith. "Not the Inquisition of Seville, nor the German Vehmgericht, nor the Secret Societies of Italy, were ever able to put a more formidable machinery in motion than that which cast a cloud over the State of Utah."

Insuperable — an obstacle or difficulty which is impossible to overcome. In the first part of *The Adventure of Wisteria Lodge*, Holmes tries to make sense of the statement of Mr. Scott Eccles and the murder of Mr. Aloysius Garcia. "I have not all my facts yet, but I do not think there are any insuperable difficulties. Still, it is an error to argue in front of your data."

Interposed — an interruption between a thought, story or objects. Holmes interrupts Openshaw to question and comment on the narrative in *The Five Orange Pips*. "One moment," Holmes interposed, "your statement is, I foresee, one of the most remarkable to which I have ever listened."

Inviolate — free or safe from injury or violation and spoken by the King of Bohemia in relation to Irene Adler's vow to not use the photograph to cause a scandal at the

King's wedding in *A Scandal in Bohemia*. "I know that her word is inviolate. The photograph is now as safe as if it were in the fire."

Iodoform — an antiseptic compound used for minor skin diseases and one of the observations which Holmes makes to deduce Watson's return to medical practice in *A Scandal in Bohemia*. "...if a gentleman walks into my rooms smelling of iodoform, with a black mark of nitrate of silver upon his right forefinger, and a bulge on the right side of his top-hat to show where he has secreted his stethoscope, I must be dull, indeed, if I do not pronounce him to be an active member of the medical profession."

Irascible — somebody who is easily irritated and provoked to anger. It served as a warning to Holmes and Watson from Mr. Bennett to be wary of Professor Presbury in *The Adventure of the Creeping Man*. "'That is excellent,' said Mr. Bennett. 'I warn you, however, that the professor is irascible and violent at times.'"

Isonomy — sometimes written as Sonomy in the American publication. Isonomy was an actual, and rather famous, thoroughbred racehorse and sire. This reference added gravitas and realism to the missing Wessex Cup favourite in *Silver Blaze*. "'Silver Blaze,' said he, 'is from the Isonomy stock, and holds as brilliant a record as his famous ancestor.'"

Ivernian — refers to somebody of Irish descent or something which is pertaining to Ireland. In *The Hound of the Baskervilles*, Watson admires the Devonshire countryside and remarks that he has never met a native of Devon who didn't love it also. He is corrected by Dr Mortimer who explains that it is as much to do with the breed of man and goes on to describe the features of Sir Charles Baskerville. "Poor Sir Charles's head was of a very rare type, half Gaelic, half Ivernian in its characteristics."

Jack-in-office — a person who is seen as self-important even though he is employed in only a minor official position. Holmes is called this, amongst other unsavoury names, by a very angry Dr Grimesby Roylott in *The Adventure of the Speckled Band*. "'I have heard of you before. You are Holmes, the meddler.' My friend smiled. 'Holmes, the busybody!' His smile broadened. 'Holmes, the Scotland Yard Jack-in-office!' Holmes chuckled heartily."

Jean Paul — this is a reference to the writer Jean Paul Richter who was a German author of witty novels and stories and who is paraphrased by Holmes in *The Sign of Four*, as he notes to Watson how the writer argues a power of comparison as being proof of nobility. "He makes one curious but profound remark. It is that the chief proof of man's real greatness lies in his perception of his own smallness."

Jemmy — a type of crowbar used by burglars to force things open. This makes up part of Holmes' burglary kit in *The Adventure of Charles Augustus Milverton* as he tries, quickly and quietly, to crack Milverton's safe. "Turning up the cuffs of his dress-coat — he had placed his overcoat on a chair —Holmes laid out two drills, a jemmy, and several skeleton keys."

Jezail — was a simple, cheap and sometimes handmade muzzle-loading gun and was the primary weapon used by the Afghan warriors against the British troops in the Anglo-Afghan war in the mid-1800s. Watson mentions it as he complains about the ache in his leg whilst nursing a bruised ego from the criticism levelled at him by Holmes in *A Sign of Four*. "I made no remark, however, but sat nursing my wounded leg. I had a Jezail bullet through it sometime before, and, though it did not prevent me from walking, it ached wearily at every change of the weather."

Jocosely — to be humorous or jokingly playful. Such is the mood of Jefferson Hope in the closing of his account in part two of *A Study in Scarlet*. Hope explains to Holmes why he did not collect the ring which was found at the scene of the murder himself but, rather, sent an accomplice. "The prisoner winked at my friend jocosely. "I can tell my own secrets," he said, "but I don't get other people into trouble"

Journal de Genève — a Swiss, French-language, regional daily newspaper which is mentioned in *The Final Problem* by Watson as he finally writes the truth about the demise of his intimate friend, Sherlock Holmes. After some scathing letters written by Colonel James Moriarty (Professor Moriarty's brother), he wants to set the record straight. "As far as I know, there have been only three accounts in the public press: that in the Journal de Genève on May 6th, 1891, the Reuter's despatch in the English papers on May 7th, and finally the recent letter to which I have alluded."

Journeys end in lovers' meeting — is a quote from the Shakespeare comedy *Twelfth Night* and is used by Holmes a couple of times in his narratives. His tone is jovial when using it after he has bested Sebastian Moran in *The Adventure of the Empty House* after he attempts to murder Holmes. "'Ah, Colonel!' said Holmes, arranging his rumpled collar; "journeys end in lovers' meetings,' as the old play says.'"

Kindled — to become impassioned, aroused or excited as did Sir George Burnwell when he learned of the golden treasure in *The Adventure of the Beryl Coronet* and so manipulated Burnwell's niece Mary to his evil will. "She told him of the coronet. His wicked lust for gold kindled at the news, and he bent her to his will."

Kneller — Sir Godfrey Kneller was the most renowned portrait painter in the late 17th and early 18th centuries. He painted noblemen, kings and is best known for his series of paintings of Isaac Newton. In *The Hound of the Baskervilles*, Holmes is drawn to the portraits which hang in Baskerville Hall and becomes unusually excited as he attempts to identify the painter behind the faces. "'I know what is good when I see it, and I see it now. That's a Kneller, I'll swear, that lady in the blue silk over yonder, and the stout gentleman with the wig ought to be a Reynolds. They are all family portraits, I presume?'"

Lady Day — March 25th, the Feast of the Annunciation for the "Lady" who is the Virgin Mary. This is the day that Dr Percy Trevelyan moved into practice financed by Mr. Blessington in *The Adventure of the Resident Patient*. "It ended in my moving into the house next Lady Day, and starting in practice on very much the same conditions as he had suggested."

Landau — a horse-drawn, four-wheeled, enclosed carriage with a removable front cover used many times in the Canon. Here it is used by Irene Adler as she instructs one to follow the coach of Godfrey Norton in *A Scandal in Bohemia*. "I was just wondering whether I should not do well to follow them when up the lane came a neat little landau, the coachman with his coat only half-buttoned."

Languid — the act of showing little interest, exertion or expending any effort in something. This is how Holmes appears to treat the case of Mr. John Hector McFarlane in The *Adventure of the Norwood Builder*. "The case has certainly some points of interest," said he, in his languid fashion. "May I ask, in the first place, Mr. McFarlane, how it is that you are still at liberty, since there appears to be enough evidence to justify your arrest?"

Languor — a contented tiredness or inactivity which is pleasurable. This is how Watson describes the relaxed and happy swing of Sherlock Holmes' moods between peaceful enjoyment, in this case during a violin concert, and the intensity when he is on a case. "The swing of his nature took him from extreme languor to devouring energy."

Lassitude — a state of weariness, listlessness or lack of energy. It is how Watson describes the curious man at the Bar of Gold opium den in *The Man with the Twisted Lip*. "...opium pipe dangling down from between his knees, as though it had dropped in sheer lassitude from his fingers."

Lath — as in a lath-and-plaster partition. A lath is a thin flat strip of wood, usually used to form a foundation for the plaster of a wall. *In The Adventure of the Norwood Builder*, it was part of the construction which was found in the house of Mr. Jonas Oldacre. "A lath-and-plaster partition had been run across the passage six feet from the end, with a door cunningly concealed in it."

Laudanum — often a 10 percent solution of opium powder in alcohol and said to have been the start of Isa Whitney's unfortunate drug habit in *The Man with the Twisted Lip* "...having read De Quincey's description of his dreams and sensations, he had drenched his tobacco with laudanum in an attempt to produce the same effects."

Legation — a legate is a diplomatic minister ranked below an ambassador (who traditionally was the representative of a monarchy rather than of a republic – a distinction no longer observed) as well as also being the official residence of a diplomatic minister. In *His Last Bow*, we learn of Baron Von Herling being flagged by a large car. "One of these was his present companion, Baron Von Herling, the chief secretary of the legation, whose huge 100-horse-power Benz car was blocking the country lane as it waited to waft its owner back to London."

Le mauvais goût mène au crime — translated as 'bad taste leads to crime' and is a quote from the writer Marie-Henri Beyle who was better known by his pen name Stendhal. It is quoted by Mr. Thaddeus Sholto after the gratitude Mary Morstan shows him in defending her father's honour and sending her a valuable pearl each month from their treasure trove. "...it would have been such bad taste to have treated a young lady in so scurvy a fashion. 'Le mauvais goût mène au crime.' The French have a very neat way of putting these things."

Les Huguenots — this is a French opera by Giacomo Meyerbeer and was said to have been lavish in its execution and its high drama, and its impressive musical arrangement would have been typical of the Grand Opera genre. The plot revolves around the love between the Catholic Valentine and the Protestant Raoul and is set during the time leading up to the St. Bartholomew's Day Massacre in 1572. In *The Hound of the Baskervilles*, Holmes, after an exhaustive few cases and the tying up of the loose ends of the Baskerville Hall case, invites Watson to relax with him at the opera. "And now, my dear Watson, we have had some weeks of severe work, and for one evening, I think, we may turn our thoughts into more pleasant channels. I have a box for 'Les Huguenots.' Have you heard the De Reszkes?"

L'homme c'est rien, l'oeuvre c'est tout, — "The man is nothing, the work is all." A quote by Gustave Flaubert, a leading French writer in the literary realism movement. The quote is used by Holmes in *A Case of Identity* to, once again, explain how his life revolves around his work of solving problems to stave off his listlessness. "'L'homme c'est rien — l'oeuvre c'est tout,' as Gustave Flaubert wrote to George Sand.'"

Life-preserver — is a slang word for a weapon. This is usually a short stick with a weighted head to make a blow more devastating for the victim. It was such a weapon which Oberstein used to lash out at Cadogan West in *The Adventure of the Bruce-Partington Plans.* "Oberstein had a short life-preserver. He always carried it with him. As West forced his way after us into the house, Oberstein struck him on the head. The blow was a fatal one."

Lineament — distinctive and characterful facial features such as those which described the cyclist who flew past Holmes and Watson in *The Adventure of the Priory School.* "Amid a rolling cloud of dust I caught a glimpse of a pale, agitated face — a face with horror in every lineament, the mouth open, the eyes staring wildly in front."

Lithotypes — are prints made from an etched surface or printing plates made from substances such as shellac. They are mentioned by Holmes in *The Sign of Four*, as he reveals to Watson some of the many monographs he has written. "Here, too, is a curious little work upon the influence of a trade upon the form of the hand, with lithotypes of the hands of slaters, sailors, corkcutters, compositors, weavers, and diamond-polishers."

Locus standi — literally translated from the Latin as 'a place of standing' it refers to something being actionable or having the right to be brought to a court, as uttered by Holmes in the final passages of *The Adventure of the Copper Beeches*. "...we had best escort Miss Hunter back to Winchester, as it seems to me that our locus standi now is rather a questionable one."

Logician — a person whose topic of scholarly study is logic. Sherlock Holmes writes in his article *The Book of Life* about the ability to follow a logical chain of thought to arrive at the solution to a problem. It is via this article that Dr Watson finally comes to know the deductive powers of Sherlock Holmes (although not before calling the writer of the article an "armchair lounger" before he realises that Holmes indeed wrote the article). "'From a drop of water' said the writer, 'a logician could infer the possibility of an Atlantic or a Niagara without having seen or heard one or the other.'"

Low water — a situation where a person finds himself in difficulty or at the point of his least prosperity and success. In *The Sign of Four*, Holmes has been asked to deduce what he can from a watch given to him by Watson who is then startled by just how much he deduces. Part of the deduction is that poor Watson's brother has spent his time being in and out of financial difficulty which is indicated by the pawnbroker numbers etched into the case. "There are no less than four such numbers visible to my lens on the inside of this case. Inference, — that your brother was often at low water."

Lumber-room — a room where disused or bulky and awkwardly shaped things are kept, often in the loft (attic) of a house. At 221b Baker Street the lumber-room is filled with Holmes' collection of things which may come in useful as mentioned in *The Adventure of the Six Napoleons*. "Holmes spent the evening in rummaging among the files of the old daily papers with which one of our lumber-rooms was packed."

Magnum opus — translated from the Latin as 'great work', it refers to a work of literature, music or art which is thought of as the best and most important that the creator has ever, or will ever, produce. Bereft of his assistant, Professor Coram laments not being able to finish his greatest work in *The Adventure of the Golden Pince-Nez*. "That is my magnum opus — the pile of papers on the side table yonder. It is my analysis of the documents found in the Coptic monasteries of Syria and Egypt, a work which will cut deep at the very foundations of revealed religion."

Malefactor — another name for a person who commits a crime and, in *The Final Problem*, it is how Professor Moriarty is introduced to Watson by Holmes "For years past I have continually been conscious of some power behind the malefactor, some deep organizing power which forever stands in the way of the law, and throws its shield over the wrong-doer."

Malodorous — something which has a terrible smell or offensive odour, much like some of the experiments Holmes conducts. As Watson writes in *The Adventure of the Dying Detective*, "His incredible untidiness, his addiction to music at strange hours, his occasional revolver practice within doors, his weird and often malodorous scientific experiments, and the atmosphere of violence and danger which hung around him made him the very worst tenant in London."

Malplaquet — The Battle of Malplaquet, 1709, one of the main battles during the War of the Spanish Succession. It is where British and Austrian troops won a victory over the French near the village of Malplaquet in northern France. In *The Adventure of the Reigate Squire*, the date of the battle was to be found above the door of the Cunninghams' home. "We passed the pretty cottage where the murdered man had lived, and walked up an oak-lined avenue to the fine old Queen Anne house, which bears the date of Malplaquet upon the lintel of the door."

Malay — used to describe Austronesian people, predominantly inhabiting the Malay Peninsula. Watson writes about how he is approached by a man as he enters The Bar of Gold opium den in *The Man with the Twisted Lip*. "As I entered, a sallow Malay attendant had hurried up with a pipe for me and a supply of the drug, beckoning me to an empty berth."

Manorial — a landed estate, originally associated with a feudal lordship and the legal rights and economic powers of the Lord of the Manor. This would consist of lands within an estate in which the lord would have privileges, rents, fees and contributions from the peasants. Manorial law, to be explored in the manorial courts, dealt with matters arising from the legalities of the lord and his manor. It is referred to in *The Hound of the Baskervilles*, by

Watson's temporary neighbour, Mr. Frankland of Lafter Hall, who seems to amuse himself by becoming embroiled in legal disputes and battles. In his first letter to Holmes, Watson writes to tell him about this character. "He is learned in old manorial and communal rights, and he applies his knowledge sometimes in favour of the villagers of Fernworthy and sometimes against them, so that he is periodically either carried in triumph down the village street or else burned in effigy, according to his latest exploit."

Mantle — a loose sleeveless shawl which was worn by women and used frequently throughout the Canon. Here it is worn by Effie Munro in *The Adventure of the Yellow Face*. "I was dimly conscious that something was going on in the room, and gradually became aware that my wife had dressed herself and was slipping on her mantle and her bonnet."

Marengo — the Battle of Marengo. A French victory of Napoleon's campaign in Italy close to a village called Marengo. Napoleon crossed the Alps in order to defeat and capture an Austrian army and, thanks to this victory, Italy returned to the control of the French. In *The Adventure of the Abbey Grange*, Holmes recalls the battle and uses it as a metaphor for the case. "We have not yet met our Waterloo, Watson, but this is our Marengo, for it begins in defeat and ends in victory. I should like now to have a few words with the nurse Theresa."

Mare's-nest — an exciting discovery that turns out to be an illusion, implying foolish gullibility. In *The Sign of Four*, Holmes uses the term to describe the case of the murder of Bartholomew Sholto and the false trail which Mr. Athelney Jones is heading down. "We shall work the case out independently, and leave this fellow Jones to exult over any mare's-nest which he may choose to construct."

Martinet — in military terms this is a person who is a strict disciplinarian. In *The Adventure of the Blanched Soldier*, James M. Dodd describes Colonel Emsworth to Sherlock Holmes who tells this story. "He is a hard nail, is Colonel Emsworth. The greatest martinet in the Army in his day, and it was a day of rough language, too."

Martini bullet — is a reference to the projectiles fired from a Martini–Henry single-shot rifle which was used by the British forces from around the 1870s and continued to be in service until the end of the World War I. As Holmes continues to trail the murderer of Bartholomew Sholto in *The Sign of Four*, he finds a pouch of the poison darts and warns Watson of their deadly powers. "'There is the less fear of you or me finding one in our skin before long. I would sooner face a Martini bullet, myself.'"

Maxillary curve — the curve of the maxillae, the jaw (in mammals the upper jaw). *In The Hound of the Baskervilles*, Dr Mortimer is astounded, as is the rest of the room, at the speed and accuracy with which Holmes can identify the newspaper and the article from which the cut-out words in

97

the threatening letter sent to Sir Henry Baskerville were taken. Explaining the reasoning behind his conclusion, he compares his speciality with that of Dr Mortimer and asks him how he would identify two men from two races. "...that is my special hobby. The differences are obvious. The supra-orbital crest, the facial angle, the maxillary curve..."

Menage — a word used to describe the members of a household and uttered by Holmes in *The Adventure of the Solitary Cyclist* as he mulls over the curiosities of the case. "What sort of a menage is it which pays double the market price for a governess, but does not keep a horse although six miles from the station? Odd, Watson — very odd!"

Mendicants — another name for a street beggar, in this case the beggar, Hugh Boone, in *The Man with the Twisted Lip* who makes a profitable living from quoting great works as he begs for money. "a pair of very penetrating dark eyes, which present a singular contrast to the colour of his hair, all mark him out from amid the common crowd of mendicants and so, too, does his wit, for he is ever ready with a reply to any piece of chaff which may be thrown at him by the passers-by."

Meretricious — apparently attractive but having no real value. Holmes uses this in *The Adventure of the Crooked Man* to describe Watson's depiction of him in his short stories. He explains that what he, and his readers, may find amazing and mesmerising is just simple inference. "The same may be said, my dear fellow, for the effect of some of these little sketches of yours, which is entirely meretricious, depending as it does upon your retaining in your own hands some factors in the problem which are never imparted to the reader."

Métier — in French, a person's profession or occupation. In English it may refer to an area in which one is particularly skilled. Talking during their train ride in *The Boscombe Valley Mystery*, Holmes demonstrates that his observation skills are superior to that of Lestrade by drawing conclusions about Watson. He reveals that his morning shave tells him that his bedroom window is on the right-hand side. "I only quote this as a trivial example of observation and inference. Therein lies my métier, and it is just possible that it may be of some service in the investigation which lies before us."

Miasmatic — a noxious or infectious gas, often a product of a swamp or similar wetland and believed to cause disease, e.g., malaria and typhoid fever. A vapour in the atmosphere which pollutes it. As Holmes and Watson explore the moor in their attempt to find the murderous Mr. Stapleton in *The Hound of the Baskervilles*, they follow a guide of plants which mark the way, safely, through the stinking bog. "Rank reeds and lush, slimy water-plants sent an odour of decay and a heavy miasmatic vapour onto our faces, while a false step plunged us more than once thigh-deep into the dark, quivering mire..."

Minstrel's gallery — this is a type of balcony which is sometimes found at one end of great halls and is just big enough for a small group of musicians (minstrels) to play for guests. It is usually located at the end of the hall opposite the high table of the host and his important guests. Watson explores Baskerville Hall in *The Hound of the Baskervilles*, and describes the gloomy dining hall where he and Sir James are sitting for dinner. "At one end a minstrel's gallery overlooked it. Black beams shot across above our heads, with a smoke-darkened ceiling beyond them."

Mitral valve — this is the valve found between the left atrium and the left ventricle of the heart, and the thing which is giving Mr. Thaddeus Sholto some cause for worry in *The Sign of Four*, "Might I ask you would you have the kindness? I have grave doubts as to my mitral valve, if you would be so very good. The aortic I may rely upon, but I should value your opinion upon the mitral."

Moidore — this is an archaic term for a Portuguese gold coin and comes from the phrase *moeda d'ouro*", which means gold coin or money of gold. The moidore was used as currency around the world, including Western Europe and the West Indies. In England at the time of the narrative, the coin would have been worth about 27 shillings. In *The Sign of Four*, Jonathan Small tells how he imagined his return to England as a rich man when he had collected his share of the Agra treasure. "...how my folk would stare when they saw their ne'er do-well coming back with his pockets full of gold moidores."

Monograph — a detailed piece of writing on a single specific topic of which Sherlock Holmes has written many. His most well-known monograph is his major work on ash which he mentions to Watson in *A Study in Scarlet*. "I have made a special study of cigar ashes – in fact, I have written a monograph upon the subject. I flatter myself that I can distinguish at a glance the *ash* of any known brand, either of *cigar* or of tobacco."

Monomaniac — a person obsessed with one thing to an excitable and unnaturally enthusiastic level. Part of Mr. Hartherley's stubborn logic for not trusting the woman who tries to warn him of impending danger in *The Adventure of the Engineer's Thumb*. "This woman might, for all I knew, be a monomaniac."

Monsieur Bertillon — another reference here to Alphonse Bertillon, the French police officer who also worked as a biometrics researcher. He created a system of measurements of body parts and physical features, especially the head and face, to produce a detailed description of an individual. He also invented the mug shot. In *The Hound of the Baskervilles*, Holmes is a little put out, after much praising of his skills and his skull by Dr James Mortimer, to be called the second highest expert in Europe. "May I inquire who has the honour to be the first?' asked Holmes with some asperity. 'To the man of precisely scientific mind the work of Monsieur Bertillon must always appeal strongly.' 'Then had you not better consult him?'"

Morass —a bog, swamp, marsh or area of soft and muddy ground. In *The Hound of the Baskervilles,* Watson writes about his evening stroll out on the dark, rainy and windy moor as he contemplates the fate of the convict and anybody else who is stuck out in the terrible conditions.

Mousseline de soie — a semi-transparent silk muslin material often used to make house coats and wraps. It is used by Watson to describe the garment worn by Mrs. St, Clair upon their first meeting in *The Man with the Twisted Lip.* "...a little blonde woman stood in the opening, clad in some sort of light mousseline de soie, with a touch of fluffy pink chiffon at her neck and wrists."

Muffler — a warm woollen scarf and one of the signs that Brunton the butler had been in the cellar, and up to no good, in *The Adventure of the Musgrave Ritual.* "'By Jove!' cried my client. 'That's Brunton's muffler. I have seen it on him, and could swear to it. What has the villain been doing here?'"

Mulatto — an out-dated name considered disparaging and offensive given to a person of mixed white and black parentage. Used throughout the story but also written in a newspaper article stating that Baynes had caught the supposed killer in the second part of *The Adventure of Wisteria Lodge.* "...two tradespeople who have caught a glimpse of him through the window, was a man of most remarkable appearance — being a huge and hideous mulatto, with yellowish features..."

Mullioned — describes windows with vertical parts made of wood or stone giving them a panelled look and found, particularly, in Gothic architecture. This is how Holmes describes his feelings about Reginald Musgrave in *The Adventure of the Musgrave Ritual*, "I never looked at his pale, keen face or the poise of his head without associating him with grey archways and mullioned windows and all the venerable wreckage of a feudal keep."

Munificent — something which displays great generosity. Much like Colonel Lysander Stark's offer of fifty guineas for just an hour of work to Mr. Hatherley in *The Adventure of the Engineer's Thumb*. "'The work appears to be light and the pay munificent.'"

Napoleons — is a colloquial term for a former French gold coin some of which are the object of desire for the third smartest criminal in London, John Clay in *The Adventure of the Red-Headed League*. As the bank chairman, Mr. Merryweather explains, "We had occasion some months ago to strengthen our resources and borrowed for that purpose 30,000 napoleons from the Bank of France."

Nettled — to be irritated or annoyed at a person and how Holmes reacts in *The Adventure of the Dancing Men* when Watson calls his impressive deduction, simple. "'Quite so!' said he, a little nettled. 'Every problem becomes very childish when once it is explained to you.'"

Newgate Calendar — a monthly publication issued from the mid-17th to the 18th century which dealt with notorious crimes and executions. It was produced by the Keeper of Newgate Prison but the title was taken up by other publishers who wished to write about crime and criminals. In *The Adventure of the Three Garridebs*, Holmes mentions the publication to Watson when he reveals the true identity of Nathan Garrideb to be that of "Killer" Evans. "Ah, it is not part of your profession to carry about a portable Newgate Calendar in your memory. I have been down to see friend Lestrade at the Yard."

Niggardly — not as offensive a term as it sounds, this simply means a person who is ungenerous or mean with money or time or a person who gives little and begrudgingly. Speaking about the matter of a reward, The Duke of Holdernesse becomes impatient with Holmes in *The Adventure of the Priory School*, "'Yes, yes,' cried the Duke, impatiently. 'If you do your work well, Mr. Sherlock Holmes, you will have no reason to complain of niggardly treatment.'"

Nihilist — is a person who rejects moral and religious ideologies and principles. It also formed part of the Russian movement in the 1860s which rejected all authorities and used violence to bring about political change. It is whom Mr. Morse Hudson believes is responsible for the vandalism of the busts in *The Adventure of the Six Napoleons*. "'Disgraceful, sir! A Nihilist plot, that's what I make it. No one but an Anarchist would go about breaking statues. Red republicans, that's what I call 'em.'"

Nitrate of silver — this can be used for a variety of tasks, from removing verrucas to curing sexually transmitted diseases such as gonorrhoea and syphilis. It is one of the observations which Holmes makes when he deduces Watson's return to medical practice in *A Scandal in Bohemia*: "...if a gentleman walks into my rooms smelling of iodoform, with a black mark of nitrate of silver upon his right forefinger, and a bulge on the right side of his top-hat to show where he has secreted his stethoscope, I must be dull, indeed, if I do not pronounce him to be an active member of the medical profession."

Norfolk jacket — a specific style of jacket with box pleats which is usually made from tweed. In *The Adventure of Black Peter*, this is the jacket worn by the intruder who is being watched by Holmes, Watson and Hopkins. "He was dressed like a gentleman, in Norfolk jacket and knickerbockers, with a cloth cap upon his head."

Nostrum — a medicine made or prepared by the person selling it, especially one that is considered to have no effect. In *The Sign of Four*, as poor Watson contemplates how the soon-to-be-rich Mary Morstan will become 'out of his league' as it were, he finds he only half listens to the hypochondria of Mr. Thaddeus Sholto. "...I was dreamily conscious that he was pouring forth interminable trains of symptoms, and imploring information as to the composition and action of innumerable quack nostrums, some of which he bore about in a leather case in his pocket."

Nous verrons — French for "We will see" which is said to Lestrade in the cab ride after Holmes deduces and describes the killer much to the amusement of the "facts over inference" detective inspector in *The Boscombe Valley Mystery*. "Nous verrons," answered Holmes calmly. "You work your own method, and I shall work mine."

Obliquity of the ecliptic — this is the angle of inclination of the plane of the Earth's equator to the plane of the Earth's revolution around the sun. This produces the relative tilt of its polar axis which causes annual seasons. Just one of the conversation topics between Holmes and Watson at the start of *The Adventure of the Greek Interpreter*. "...the conversation, which had roamed in a desultory, spasmodic fashion from golf clubs to the causes of the change in the obliquity of the ecliptic"

Obtrude — when something becomes intrusive or unwelcome in a very obvious and noticeable way. In *The Sign of Four*, poor Watson battles with his emotions and his gentlemanly ways when it comes to Mary Morstan. He yearns to tell her how he feels during their cab ride, but is prevented from doing so because she is vulnerable and soon to be very rich. "It was to take her at a disadvantage, to obtrude love upon her at such a time."

Omne ignotum pro magnifico — translated from the Latin, "the unknown always passes for the marvellous," and is a quote taken from the book *The Agricola* written by Roman historian Tacitus. The phrase is uttered by Holmes in *The Adventure of the Red-Headed League* after Mr. Jabez Wilson plays down his astonishing deductions when

Holmes explains his methods, "'I begin to think, Watson,' said Holmes, 'that I make a mistake in explaining. 'Omne ignotum pro magnifico,' you know, and my poor little reputation, such as it is, will suffer shipwreck if I am so candid.'"

Opalescent — describes something that shows many shifting colours against a dark or pale background, an item that is almost shimmering. The reference here is to the gemstone opal, a mineral that presents a shimmering, often multi-coloured appearance in light. It was used by Watson in *The Adventure of the Abbey Grange*, to describe a cab ride to Charing Cross Station at an unearthly early hour. "The first faint winter's dawn was beginning to appear, and we could dimly see the occasional figure of an early workman as he passed us, blurred and indistinct in the opalescent London reek."

Ostler — a groom or stablehand, often applied to a person who is hired to look after the horses of people staying at an inn or public house. In *A Scandal in Bohemia*, Holmes talks about getting in with the "horsey" lot to gain information. "I lent the ostlers a hand in rubbing down their horses, and received in exchange twopence, a glass of half and half, two fills of shag tobacco, and as much information as I could desire about Miss Adler."

Outré — something outlandish, grotesque or unusual. Used in *A Study in Scarlet* by Sherlock Holmes as he explains to Lestrade, Gregson and Watson his methods for unravelling the Lauriston garden murders. "This murder would have been infinitely more difficult to unravel had the body of the victim been simply found lying in the roadway without any of those outré and sensational accompaniments which have rendered it remarkable."

Ouvrier — a French name for a blue-collar worker, one who does manual labour or unskilled work. Such a man is described by Watson in *The Disappearance of Lady Frances Carfax* as coming to his aid during his attack in the street but little does he expect it to be Holmes in disguise. "His hand was on my throat and my senses were nearly gone before an unshaven French ouvrier in a blue blouse darted out from a cabaret opposite, with a cudgel in his hand, and struck my assailant a sharp crack over the forearm..."

Pagination — is a sequence of numbers on the pages of a book. In *The Valley of Fear*, Holmes and Watson attempt to solve the book code puzzle which has been sent by Porlock, but the key to the code has been discarded after suspicion was aroused in Moriarty. Watson suggests that the book could be The Bible, but this is quickly disregarded by Holmes. "'Besides, the editions of Holy Writ are so numerous that he could hardly suppose that two copies would have the same pagination. This is clearly a book which is standardized.'"

Palimpsest — a piece of writing material, generally parchment or paper, that is reused by scraping off or erasing the original text so that the material can be used again. In *The Adventure of the Golden Pince-Nez*, Watson describes the companionable quiet in which he and Holmes sat. "Holmes and I sat together in silence all the evening, he engaged with a powerful lens deciphering the remains of the original inscription upon a palimpsest, I deep in a recent treatise upon surgery."

Palladio — Andrea Palladio was a 16th century Italian architect of Venice, influenced by Greek and Roman architecture. Palladio's work was strongly based on the symmetry of these formal classical temple structures.

esteemed household name looking to borrow £50,000 in *The Adventure of the Beryl Coronet.* "'I should be happy to advance it without further parley from my own private purse...'"

Paroxysm — a sudden outburst of excitement or action. In *The Adventure of the Stock Broker's Clerk*, Holmes suddenly comes to life when he is reminded of the newspaper which Mr. Arthur Pinner was reading before his attempt to end his own life. "'The paper! Of course!' yelled Holmes, in a paroxysm of excitement. 'Idiot that I was! I thought so much of our visit that the paper never entered my head for an instant.'" The word can also be found in *The Adventure of the Norwood Builder* as Holmes tries to fight facts with his gut instincts, "'And yet—and yet' — he clenched his thin hands in a paroxysm of conviction — 'I know it's all wrong. I feel it in my bones.'"

Partie carré — a term meaning four people (usually two men and two women) and is used by Holmes to describe the group of men who are lying in wait at the bank vault to catch the thief red-handed in *The Adventure of the Red-Headed League.* "I had brought a pack of cards in my pocket, and I thought that, as we were a Partie carré, you might have your rubber after all."

Pawky — describes a person with a tricky, sly, cynical, or mocking sense of humour. This phrase is directed towards Watson in *The Valley of Fear*, as Holmes expects, and then prematurely admonishes him, for a compliment about his reputation when placed next to that of Professor James Moriarty. Already a little annoyed with him and his ego, Watson goes on to demonstrate that he had no intention of complimenting Holmes and so attempts to put him in his place. A fact which Holmes finds rather amusing. "'A touch! A distinct touch!' cried Holmes. 'You are developing a certain unexpected vein of pawky humour, Watson, against which I must learn to guard myself.'"

Pawnees — Pawnees are an Amerindian or Native American people, mentioned in association with the Blackfeet people in part two of *A Study in Scarlet*. "There are no inhabitants of this land of despair. A band of Pawnees or of Blackfeet may occasionally traverse it in order to reach other hunting-grounds, but the hardiest braves are glad to lose sight of those awesome plains and to find themselves once more upon their prairies." (See also Blackfeet.)

Peached — 'Peach' is a slang word meaning to inform on somebody, or to 'grass them up'. In *The Adventure of the Mazarin Stone*, Holmes bombards Count Negretto Sylvius with the evidence against him and the theft of the stone and how many have spoken up regarding his actions. "I have the commissionaire who saw you near the case. I have Ikey Sanders, who refused to cut it up for you. Ikey has peached, and the game is up."

Pea-jacket — (or pea coat) is a double-breasted, short overcoat made of very coarse wool and commonly worn by sailors. Holmes sports the coat in a disguise as he wakes up Watson before he starts his undercover investigation in *The Sign of Four.* "In the early dawn I woke with a start, and was surprised to find him standing by my bedside, clad in a rude sailor dress with a pea-jacket, and a coarse red scarf round his neck."

Peine forte et dure — translated as 'strong and harsh punishment' and is a reference to a form of torture where a person who was unwilling to communicate (stood mute) or make a plea of guilty or not guilty would be tortured, often having large weights, commonly stones, gradually piled onto their chest until they either spoke or died. The phrase was directed at Mr. Barker in *The Valley of Fear* as he is presented with evidence of a cover-up in regards to the supposed murder of Mr. Douglas. Barker is, however, unwilling to cooperate with Holmes or any of the authorities within the room. "The proceedings seemed to have come to a definite end so far as he was concerned; for one had only to look at that granite face to realize that no peine forte et dure would ever force him to plead against his will."

Pellucid — something which is as clear as glass, transparent or translucent. This is how Holmes describes the pool of water which attracted swimmers on the beach near his small home in Sussex which held a deadly secret *in The Adventure of The Lion's Mane.* "It was to this part that a swimmer would naturally go, for it formed a beautiful pellucid green pool as clear as crystal. A line of rocks lay above it at the base of the cliff, and along this I led the way."

Penang-lawyer — a walking stick made from the stem of an East Asiatic dwarf palm or a Malacca palm as used by Fitzroy Simpson, the murder suspect in *Silver Blaze*. "…his stick, which was a Penang-lawyer weighted with lead, was just such a weapon as might, by repeated blows, have inflicted the terrible injuries to which the trainer had succumbed."

Pensions — in this context, Holmes is referring to a small and relatively inexpensive hotel, often offering a meal or two daily, which can be found in France and other European countries. He uses it in *The Disappearance of Lady Frances Carfax* as he relays to Watson the danger of the drifting woman. "She is lost, as often as not, in a maze of obscure pensions and boarding houses. She is a stray chicken in a world of foxes. When she is gobbled up, she is hardly missed."

Penurious — miserly and mean, describing a person who is stingy or who is poor and lacks resources. As Watson is sent to deputise for Holmes in *The Adventure of the Retired Colourman*, he relates to him the dwelling of their latest client Mr. Josiah Amberey. "I think it would interest you, Holmes. It is like some penurious patrician who has sunk into the company of his inferiors."

Pince-nez — eyeglasses worn perched upon the nose, held in place by a spring arrangement that pinches the bridge of the nose. In *The Adventure of the Golden Pince-Nez*, Stanley Hopkins produces them as he describes to Holmes his findings in regards to the violent murder of **Willoughby Smith**. "From his pocket Stanley Hopkins drew a small paper packet. He unfolded it and disclosed a golden pince-nez, with two broken ends of black silk cord dangling from the end of it."

Perambulation — to walk around and or causally stroll as Watson did, looking through the shelves as Holmes slept in *The Adventure of the Dying Detective*. "Finally, in my aimless perambulation, I came to the mantelpiece. A litter of pipes, tobacco pouches, syringes, penknives, revolver-cartridges, and other debris was scattered over it."

Peremptorily — when a person leaves no chance or opportunity for an action to be denied or refused. In *The Adventure of the Second Stain*, Watson explains to his readers the current attitude of Holmes in regards to his stories being shared. "...since he has definitely retired from London and betaken himself to study and bee-farming on the Sussex Downs, notoriety has become hateful to him, and he has peremptorily requested that his wishes in this matter should be strictly observed." Also included as peremptory in *The Hound of the Baskervilles*, "Finally Stapleton turned upon his heel and beckoned in a peremptory way to his sister, who, after an irresolute glance at Sir Henry, walked off by the side of her brother."

Pertinacious — the act of being stubborn or obstinate. In *The Adventure of the Three Gables*, Isadora Klein explains to Holmes and Watson the reasons why she could not stay with Douglas Maberle. "He wanted marriage — marriage, Mr. Holmes — with a penniless commoner. Nothing less would serve him. Then he became pertinacious. Because I had given he seemed to think that I still must give, and to him only."

Petrarch — Francesco Petrarca, commonly anglicized as *Petrarch*, was an Italian scholar and poet in Renaissance Italy, who was one of the earliest humanists. Referenced by Holmes in *The Boscombe Valley Mystery* as the book he will read, in silence, until they reach their destination of the crime scene. "And now here is my pocket Petrarch, and not another word shall I say of this case until we are on the scene of action."

Pertinacity — the trait of standing firm in an opinion or a course of action. Mrs. Warren in *The Adventure of the Red Circle* was determined that Holmes take her complaint seriously. "But the landlady had the pertinacity and also the cunning of her sex. She held her ground firmly."

Pharmacopoeia — this is an official publication which contains a list of medicines along with their effects and comes from the Greek *pharmakopoiia* "art of preparing drugs." As Dr Sterndale tells of his motives, he shows to Holmes and Watson a paper packet of Devil's-foot root in *The Adventure of the Devil's Foot,* and he explains its meaning. "It has not yet found its way either into the pharmacopoeia or into the literature of toxicology. The root is shaped like a foot, half human, half goat-like; hence the fanciful name given by a botanical missionary."

Phlegmatic — a person who is utterly calm and unaffected by emotions. There can be no more apt a description of Holmes than this in *The Adventure of the Devil's Foot*: "One realized the red-hot energy which underlay Holmes's phlegmatic exterior when one saw the sudden change which came over him from the moment that he entered the fatal apartment."

Phoenician — an ancient language spoken by the inhabitants of Phoenicia and its colonies (which included the coastline of what is now northern Israel, Lebanon, Syria, and southwest Turkey). Holmes mentions them in *The Adventure of the Devil's Foot* whilst speaking of the Cornish language. "The ancient Cornish language had also arrested his attention, and he had, I remember, conceived the idea that it was akin to the Chaldean, and had been largely derived from the Phoenician traders in tin."

Pinfire revolver — a gun which uses a pinfire cartridge ammunition. This was a metallic cartridge where the compound was ignited by striking a small pin which stuck out from just above the base of it. Invented in 1830 but now obsolete. In part two of *The Adventure of Wisteria Lodge*, it is counted amongst the possessions found at the Lodge whilst looking for clues. "Odds and ends, some pipes, a few novels, two of them in Spanish, and old-fashioned pinfire

Pink 'un — a newspaper printed on pink paper, usually a publication such as The Sporting Times. It was this clue that led Holmes to know Mr. Breckinridge the poultry seller was a betting man and so used it to trick him into parting with much-needed information in *The Adventure of the Blue Carbuncle*. "When you see a man with whiskers of that cut and the 'Pink 'un' protruding out of his pocket, you can always draw him by a bet."

Plate — items such as bowls, cups or utensils made of gold or silver. Holmes inquires, in *The Adventure of the Naval Treaty*, if Mr. Phelps has any such items in his home which may be the reason for the attempted burglary. "'Do you keep plate in the house, or anything to attract burglars?' 'Nothing of value.'"

Plethoric — something which is overly large, or abundant. In *The Adventure of Charles Augustus Milverton*, this is how Holmes describes Milverton's sleeping patterns as they make their way to Appledore Towers. "On the other hand, like all these stout, little men who do themselves well, he is a plethoric sleeper."

Plover's egg — a plover is a wading bird whose mottled eggs were a delicacy in Victorian Europe and their speckled appearance is how Watson described the complexion of Miss Violet Hunter in *The Adventure of the Copper Beeches*. "She was plainly but neatly dressed, with a bright, quick face, freckled like a plover's egg."

Poe — Edgar Allan Poe, notable writer most famous for his stories of mystery and the macabre. The work referenced in *The Adventure of the Cardboard Box*, is most likely to be the detective C. Auguste Dupin who was also a figure with great detective powers. Holmes references this as Watson is astounded at what he perceives as having his mind read, especially after dismissing something similar in one of Poe's books at an early time. "I read you the passage in one of Poe's sketches in which a close reasoner follows the unspoken thoughts of his companion, you were inclined to treat the matter as a mere tour-de-force of the author."

Pole-axed — somebody who is so surprised or stunned that they are shocked into not knowing what to say or do. Thus was the reaction to the card sent to Godfrey Staunton in *The Adventure of the Missing Three-Quarter*. "He had not gone to bed and the note was taken to his room. Godfrey read it and fell back in a chair as if he had been pole-axed. The porter was so scared that he was going to fetch me."

Pollarded — describes trees that have been cut back to the trunk, or nearly so, to encourage them to develop new growth. Used in *The Valley of Fear*, Watson describes his picturesque surroundings. "We walked down the quaint village street with a row of pollarded elms on each side of it."

Polyphonic Motets of Lassus — Orlando di Lasso was a Flemish composer (whose musical style dominated European music during the Renaissance) and a primary representative of the mature polyphonic style of the Franco-Flemish school. Polyphonic music consists of two or more simultaneous lines of separate melody, as opposed to just one. In *The Adventure of the Bruce-Partington Plans*, Holmes had become engrossed upon the subject once he had figured out the pertinent details of the mystery and planned its conclusion. "I remember that during the whole of that memorable day he lost himself in a monograph which he had undertaken upon the Polyphonic Motets of Lassus."

Populus me sibilat, at mihi plaudo Ipse domi stimul ac nummos contemplar in arca — translated from the Latin to mean "The public hiss at me, but I cheer myself when in my own house I contemplate the coins in my strong-box" and it is the final phrase at the conclusion of *A Study in Scarlet*. This is Watson's way of reassuring Holmes that he will write and tell people who the true genius in crime-solving is. "'Never mind,' I answered, 'I have all the facts in my journal, and the public shall know them. In the meantime you must make yourself contented by the consciousness of success, like the Roman miser— Populus me sibilat, at mihi plaudo Ipse domi simul ac nummos contemplar in arca.'"

Porticoed — a type of house which includes a roof supported by columns or piers attached to it to form a porch. These were the kinds of houses described by Watson in *The Adventure of the Bruce-Partington Plans* as they made their way to Caulfield Gardens. "Caulfield Gardens was one of those lines of flat-faced pillared, and porticoed houses which are so prominent a product of the middle Victorian epoch in the West End of London."

Portiere — a curtain which is hung over a door or doorway and something which is used by Watson while describing his slow creep around the inside the house of Milverton in *The Adventure of Charles Augustus Milverton,* "We were in Milverton's study, and a portiere at the farther side showed the entrance to his bedroom."

Portmanteau — a leather travelling bag. Made reference to in *A Study in Scarlet* as Sherlock Holmes endeavours to explain to Lestrade and Gregson how he knew the identity of the killer. Pretending he needs a cab to take him on a journey, he slaps the cuffs on the cab man. "I was surprised to find my companion speaking as though he were about to set out on a journey, since he had not said anything to me about it. There was a small portmanteau in the room, and this he pulled out and began to strap."

Postulant — a person who is undertaking an admission into a group or order. This is usually a candidate who is seeking to join a religious order. Although already a member of the Freemen society, Jack McMurdo still has to go through the initiations of the lodge in Vermissa in *The Valley of Fear.* "He had thought to pass in without ceremony as being an initiate of Chicago; but there were particular rites in Vermissa of which they were proud, and these had to be undergone by every postulant."

Potentate — a ruler such as a monarch or a sovereign who possesses a great power. In *The Adventure of the Second Stain*, this is how the writer of the missing letter is described by Mr. Trelawney Hope. "The letter—for it was a letter from a foreign potentate—was received six days ago. It was of such importance that I have never left it in my safe."

Precipitate — a situation or an action, which is normally undesirable, which happens suddenly, unexpectedly or with force. As Watson voices his doubts over Holmes' plan to burgle Milverton's house in *The Adventure of Charles Augustus Milverton*, Holmes exclaims, "My dear fellow, I have given it every consideration. I am never precipitate in my actions, nor would I adopt so energetic and indeed so dangerous a course if any other were possible."

Precipitous — something which is dangerously steep with a high drop, a precipice. Holmes tries to map out the route taken by the missing young Lord Saltire in *The Adventure of the Priory School*. "There is a church there, you see, a few cottages, and an inn. Beyond that the hills become precipitous."

Preponderance — a quality which is greater in number or importance. As uttered by Holmes in *The Adventure of the Dancing Men*, as he walks Watson through how he worked out the stick men cipher. "The order of the English letters after E is by no means well-marked, and any preponderance which may be shown in an average of a printed sheet may be reversed in a single short sentence."

Presentiment — a feeling or an intuition about the future, more often than not, a foreboding feeling such as the one Mrs. Effie Munro had in *The Adventure of the Yellow Face* when her husband, Holmes and Watson entered the cottage to solve the mystery of the new inhabitants. "'For God's sake, don't Jack!' she cried. 'I had a presentiment that you would come this evening.'"

Prevaricate — the act of being evasive, avoiding commenting on a subject or answering a question with redirection. Holmes warns Dr Sterndale in *The Adventure of the Devil's Foot*, not to do so as he puts forward his theory of how Mortimer Tregennis was murdered. "If you prevaricate or trifle with me, I give you my assurance that the matter will pass out of my hands forever."

Privations — lacking usual comforts of life or even the basics needed for existence. In *A Study in Scarlet*, it is used to reinforce the struggle and the journey which the Mormons endured before they reached their final destination. "This is not the place to commemorate the trials and privations endured by the immigrant Mormons before they came to their final haven."

Profusion — when there is an abundance or large quantity of something. In *The Sign of Four*, Holmes hands Watson a letter which contains a large number of compliments regarding his help in solving a case involving a will. "He tossed over, as he spoke, a crumpled sheet of foreign notepaper. I glanced my eyes down it, catching a profusion of notes of admiration."

Propitious — promising better conditions or situations at a time which is more favourable. This is the suggestion made to James M. Dodd who is told to come back to see his friend Godfrey Emsworth at another time in *The Adventure of the Blanched Soldier*. "'No doubt you will renew your visit at some more propitious time.' He passed on, but when I turned, I observed that he was standing watching me, half-concealed by the laurels at the far end of the garden."

Propound — to put something forward to be considered by others. Used by Lord St. Simon, in surprise, when asked by Holmes if he has any theories regarding the disappearance of his wife in *The Adventure of the Noble Bachelor*. "Well, really, I came to seek a theory, not to propound one. I have given you all the facts."

Prussic acid — more commonly known as a solution of hydrogen cyanide. It is colourless and highly poisonous liquid with a faint smell of almonds. In the last paragraphs of *The Adventure of the Veiled Lodger*, Holmes is sent a bottle through the post with a note from the woman who was to take her own life. "I picked it up. There was a red poison label. A pleasant almondy odour rose when I opened it. "Prussic acid?" said I. "Exactly. It came by post. 'I send you my temptation. I will follow your advice.'"

Purport — the general meaning behind a person's words or actions. Used by Watson to describe the look on Miss Mary Sutherland's face when Holmes, at once, deduces her typing activity in *A Case of Identity*. "Then, suddenly realising the full purport of his words, she gave a violent start and looked up, with fear and astonishment upon her broad, good-humoured face."

Purview — scope, range, and limits of the responsibilities of employment or of a position, or of a document. In *The Adventure of the Sussex Vampire*, Holmes is sent a letter by Morrison, Morrison, and Dodd concerning the topic of vampires as enquired by their client Mr. Robert Ferguson. As this is not their area they have forwarded the enquiry to Sherlock Holmes. "As our firm specializes entirely upon the assessment of machinery the matter hardly comes within our purview, and we have therefore recommended Mr. Ferguson to call upon you and lay the matter before you."

Queer Street — although the meaning of the word "queer" has undergone many changes in its lifetime, in the 1800s it was British slang for a street where people who were very poor or in difficult circumstances lived. Almost like the British version of "Skid Row." It is a colloquial term referring to a person being in some difficulty, most commonly financial. It is used frequently in the Canon, but the last short story in which it is used is *The Adventure of Shoscombe Old Place* where Watson describes Sir Robert Norberton to Holmes. "He should have been a buck in the days of the Regency — a boxer, an athlete, a plunger on the turf, a lover of fair ladies, and, by all account, so far down Queer Street that he may never find his way back again."

Querulous — describes a whiny and complaining person who can be rather petulant. In *The Adventure of the Naval Treaty*, poor Watson is tasked with the nervy and moaning Mr. Phelps on their journey back to Baker Street. "But it was a weary day for me. Phelps was still weak after his long illness, and his misfortune made him querulous and nervous."

Quinsy — a condition which causes inflammation of the throat and also abscesses on the tonsils. This is the reason given for the soft voice of the missing man Mr. Hosmer

Angel in *A Case of Identity* as described by his distraught fiancée Miss Mary Sutherland. "Even his voice was gentle. He'd had the quinsy and swollen glands when he was young, he told me, and it had left him with a weak throat."

Rapacity — an aggressive and hungry greed felt by some people, a strong desire to have for the sake of having and wanting more. This, amongst other unflattering descriptions, was attributed to Mr. Neil Gibson in *The Problem of Thor Bridge*. "His tall, gaunt, craggy figure had a suggestion of hunger and rapacity. An Abraham Lincoln keyed to base uses instead of high ones would give some idea of the man."

Rebus — this is a puzzle in which words are represented by pictures and letters, something UK readers will be familiar with if they have watched The Big Fat Quiz of the Year or Only Connect. For example, a picture of an eye, then a heart and then the letter U would spell out I Love You. In *The Adventure of the Sussex Vampire*, there is a rebus to be found at the entrance of the Ferguson home. "The doorsteps were worn into curves, and the ancient tiles which lined the porch were marked with the rebus of a cheese and a man after the original builder."

Recalcitrants — there are people who are stubborn, resistant or defiant of authority. They can also be obstinate and difficult to manage. In part two of *A Study in Scarlet*, the author tells of the terrible fates which befall those who don't conform to the doctrine of the Mormon Church and the secret judges who dish out the punishments. "At first this vague and terrible power was exercised only upon the recalcitrants who, having embraced the Mormon faith, wished afterwards to pervert or to abandon it."

Recapitulate — to go over the same points again or to summarise. Watson talks of the Ronald Adair case in *The Adventure of the Empty House*, wanting to tell the story in his own words as well as reminding the reader of the "facts" of the case. "At the risk of telling a twice-told tale I will recapitulate the facts as they were known to the public at the conclusion of the inquest."

Recherche — something which is very rare, exotic or obscure. It appears after Holmes reads out a short list of undocumented cases to Watson. This is how he attempts to whet Watson's appetite and distract him with case files after he, boldly, suggested that Holmes clean up the flat a little in *The Adventure of the Musgrave Ritual.* "And here—ah, now, this really is something a little recherche."

Reconnoitre — is the act of looking at something with precise, military observation. In *The Adventure of the Yellow Face*, as Holmes tells Watson of his theory about Mrs. Effie Munro's strange behaviour and starts down a thread of possible explanation regarding the mysterious inhabitants of the cottage. "In this way he found the place deserted. I shall be very much surprised, however, if it still so when he reconnoitres it this evening." Holmes also uses the term as he explains the solution of the case in the second part of

The Adventure of Wisteria Lodge. "But the mulatto's heart was with it, and he was driven back to it next day, when, on reconnoitring through the window, he found policeman Walters in possession."

Red King — refers to William II of England who was also was commonly known as William Rufus and Rufus is Latin for red. He was king of England from 1087 until 1100 and is mentioned in *The Valley of Fear*, as Watson describes the Manor House of Birlstone, the scene of a terrible murder. "Part of this venerable building dates back to the time of the first crusade, when Hugo de Capus built a fortalice in the centre of the estate, which had been granted to him by the Red King."

Remonstrance — a forceful or angry protest as exclaimed by Watson during Holmes's deductions about the owner of the mysterious bowler hat in *The Adventure of the Blue Carbuncle.* "'He has, however, retained some degree of self-respect,' he continued, disregarding my remonstrance." Also used in *The Adventure of the Yellow Face*, "My lips were parted to murmur out some sleepy words of surprise or remonstrance at this untimely preparation."

Remunerative — something which is financially rewarding as explained by Mr. Alexander Holder in *The Adventure of the Beryl Coronet.* "...banking business as much depends upon our being able to find remunerative investments for our funds as upon our increasing our connection and the number of our depositors."

Reproof — something which is said to show disapproval or an expression of blame. As Holmes makes his displeasure of Mr. Neil Gibson's predatory behaviour towards Miss Grace Dunbar in *The Problem of Thor Bridge* perfectly clear. "'Well, maybe so,' said the millionaire, though for a moment the reproof had brought the old angry gleam into his eyes. 'I'm not pretending to be any better than I am.'"

Restive — The inability to keep still, especially due to being bored or dissatisfied. In *A Case of Identity*, Holmes describes the mood of Miss Sutherland at being confined to the home by her stepfather and not allowed, much like Cinderella, to socialise. "She became restive, insisted upon her rights, and finally announced her positive intention of going to a certain ball."

Reticulated — covering something over like a net or spread thread-like, over a surface. In *The Adventure of the Lion's Mane*, Holmes describes the terrible wounds on the back of poor Ian Murdoch as he crashes into his home looking for brandy. "There, crisscrossed upon the man's naked shoulder, was the same strange reticulated pattern of red, inflamed lines which had been the death-mark of Fitzroy McPherson."

Retrogression — the returning to a former, usually worse, state than before. A comment made by Holmes upon the character and habits of Mr. H. Baker, owner of the mysterious bowler hat in *The Adventure of the Blue Carbuncle*, as he deduces the man to Watson. "He had foresight, but has less now than formerly, pointing to a moral retrogression, which, when taken with the decline of his fortunes, seems to indicate some evil influence, probably drink."

Reversion — in legal terms this is when an estate is returned to the grantor or the grantor's heirs after the holder dies. It is also the right to succeed to an estate. In *The Adventure of the Dying Detective*, it is thought that this is the motivation of the terrible Culverton Smith for poisoning his nephew. "You can just see if you look at it sideways where the sharp spring like a viper's tooth emerges as you open it. I dare say it was by some such device that poor Savage, who stood between this monster and a reversion, was done to death."

Reynolds — Joshua Reynolds was one of the most famous portrait painters of the 18th century. His paintings were part of 'The Grand Style' which meant he believed portraits shouldn't be exact copies of the subject, but rather an idealised version. He is also noteworthy as he founded the Royal Academy of Arts. In *The Hound of the Baskervilles*, Holmes is drawn to the portraits which hang in Baskerville Hall and becomes unusually excited as he attempts to identify the painter behind the faces. "'I know what is good when I see it, and I see it now. That's a Kneller, I'll swear, that lady in the blue silk over yonder, and the stout gentleman with the wig ought to be a Reynolds. They are all family portraits, I presume?'"

Ribston-pippin — this is a variety of dessert apple which has a red flush to its yellow skin. This may be the reason why, in *The Adventure of Black Peter*, Watson uses the apple's appearance to describe one of the sailor men who have been summoned to Baker Street. "The first who entered was a little ribston-pippin of a man, with ruddy cheeks and fluffy white side-whiskers."

Risus sardonicus — this is a fixed, grinning expression caused by facial muscle spasms. Said to have its origins in the Mediterranean island of Sardinia, it gives the sufferer raised eyebrows and a large grin. In *The Sign of Four*, Holmes asks Watson to place his hands on the body of unfortunate Bartholomew Sholto for his medical opinion on the man's death. "Coupled with this distortion of the face, this Hippocratic smile, or 'risus sardonicus,' as the old writers called it, what conclusion would it suggest to your mind?"

Robespierre — Maximilien François Marie Isidore de Robespierre, apart from having a wonderful name, was a French lawyer and politician and one of the most influential men to be associated with the French Revolution. His main rival was Georges Danton, and during the Revolution, Danton was seen by many as an alternative to Robespierre who wanted a new Republic based on idealistic philosophy rather than his practical approach. Robespierre also went so far as to accuse Danton and his followers of treason so he could install himself and his agents in the vacancies within the government. In *The Valley of Fear*, McGinty mentions a county delegate who has power over several lodges and whom even the terrorising

McGinty finds intimidating. "Evans Pott was his name, and even the great Boss of Vermissa felt towards him something of the repulsion and fear which the huge Danton may have felt for the puny but dangerous Robespierre."

Rodney — George Brydges Rodney, 1st Baron Rodney was a British naval officer in the late 1700s who commanded during the American War of Independence. However, in *The Hound of the Baskervilles*, he is mentioned in relation to the West Indies when Holmes enquires about the man in one of the portraits which hang in the great hall. The reply identifies the subject and references Rodney's selection to command an attack on the French colony of Martinique. "'Who is the gentleman with the telescope?' 'That is Rear-Admiral Baskerville, who served under Rodney in the West Indies.'"

Rubber — Rubber bridge is a version of the card game bridge, where bonus points are awarded for scoring sufficient points to win hands in a "rubber," which is the best of three games. Poor, solemn Mr. Merryweather bemoans that he has had to miss a game for the first time in twenty-seven years in order to help solve the mystery in *The Adventure of the Red-Headed League*. "Still, I confess that I miss my rubber. It is the first Saturday night for seven-and-twenty years that I have not had my rubber." It is also mentioned in *The Adventure of the Empty House*: "It was shown that after dinner on the day of his death he had played a rubber of whist at the latter club."

Rubicund — to describe something which is red or ruddy. Used by Watson in *The Adventure of the Three Gables* to describe the inspector who greeted himself and Holmes at the Three Gables after there had been a robbery reported. "Within we met a grey old gentleman, who introduced himself as the lawyer, together with a bustling, rubicund inspector, who greeted Holmes as an old friend."

Rum — an action or a person that is odd or peculiar. This was used by Jonathan Small in *The Sign of Four*, to describe the old fort at Agra. "It is a very queer place — the queerest that ever I was in, and I have been in some rum corners, too. First of all, it is enormous in size."

Rustic — a rather insulting name for an uneducated and unsophisticated person from the country. Such a man rushes into the rooms of Holmes and Watson with news in the second part of *The Adventure of Wisteria Lodge*. "It was about five o'clock, and the shadows of the March evening were beginning to fall, when an excited rustic rushed into our room."

Rusticate — go to, live in, or spend time in the country. Used at the start of *A Study in Scarlet* by Watson as he ponders his living situation and spending a small fortune on accommodations in London. As enthusiasts of Sherlock Holmes are aware, if it hadn't been for this change in situation, Holmes and Watson might never have ended up together on their adventures. "I soon realised that I must either leave the Metropolis and rusticate somewhere in the country, or that I must make a complete alteration in my style of living."

Sagacity — showing signs of being wise, having good judgment and demonstrating a keen mental ability. So was written about the mental prowess of Inspector Lestrade in The Daily Telegraph in *The Adventure of the Norwood Builder*. "The conduct of the criminal investigation has been left in the experienced hands of Inspector Lestrade, of Scotland Yard, who is following up the clues with his accustomed energy and sagacity."

Sahib — a polite Indian term which is a form of address towards another man, the term is closely associated with the British rule in India. In *The Sign of Four*, it is used by Jonathan Small as he recounts his adventures of the Agra treasure and the two Sikh troopers who brought him into their plans. "By doing this, mark you, Sahib, his property becomes the due of those who have been true to their salt."

Sallies — a brief or sudden start into action. In *The Five Orange Pips*, John Openshaw uses it to describe the demise of his uncle after referencing a mysterious letter which contained five dried orange pips. "Well, to come to an end of the matter, Mr. Holmes, and not to abuse your patience, there came a night when he made one of those drunken sallies from which he never came back."

Salvator Rosa — was an Italian painter (as well as poet and etcher) who was well known for painting landscapes which were set within wild natural settings and were often brooding and desolate. His paintings were also an important influence on the romantic art of the 18th and 19th centuries. In *The Sign of Four*, Mr. Thaddeus Sholto shows his sensitive and artistic side to Holmes, Watson and the delicate Mary Morstan. "I may call myself a patron of the arts. It is my weakness. The landscape is a genuine Corot, and, though a connoisseur might perhaps throw a doubt upon that Salvator Rosa, there cannot be the least question about the Bouguereau. I am partial to the modern French school."

Sanguine — to be optimistic or positive, especially during difficult situations. In *The Adventure of the Cardboard Box*, Holmes uses it when recounting his deductions of the mysterious package and his hope of questioning Miss Sarah Cushing. "Then, of course, she might give us very important information, but I was not sanguine that she would."

Sapper — a soldier who is responsible for things such as repairing roads and bridges or laying and clearing mines. This was one of the rejected occupations of the stranger at the centre of Holmes and Mycroft's deductions in *The Adventure of the Greek Interpreter*. "His weight is against his being a sapper. He is in the artillery."

Sarasate — Pablo de Sarasate was a Spanish composer and violinist who was part of the "Romantic" period. In *The Adventure of the Red-Headed League*, after much thinking, Holmes proposes a break to Watson in the form of a recital. "'Sarasate plays at the St. James's Hall this afternoon,' he remarked. 'What do you think, Watson? Could your patients spare you for a few hours?'"

Saturnine — a person who has dark and gloomy features or a hint of mystery. This is how Watson describes Holmes in *The Adventure of the Mazarin Stone* as he looks around the familiar rooms of 221b Baker Street once more. "Finally, his eyes came round to the fresh and smiling face of Billy, the young but very wise and tactful page, who had helped a little to fill up the gap of loneliness and isolation which surrounded the saturnine figure of the great detective."

Sawyers — a person who saws and cuts wood for a living. In *The Sign of Four*, an excited Toby leads Holmes and Watson through the timber-yard, hot on the creosote scent. "Here the dog, frantic with excitement, turned down through the side-gate into the enclosure, where the sawyers were already at work."

Schade, dass die Natur nur einen Mensch aus dir schuf, denn zum würdigen Mann war und zum Schelmen der Stoff — translated from the German as "Alas, that Nature made only one man of you, when there was material enough for a good man and a rogue." This is the second time Holmes has quoted Johann Wolfgang von Goethe in

The Sign of Four. Here his context for using the quote is during a conversation with Watson about how lethargic having no problems or cases makes him feel. Watson comments on how these traits in another man would make him lazy, and Holmes agrees that he can be both full of energy and depleted of it all at once. "...here are in me the makings of a very fine loafer and also of a pretty spry sort of fellow. I often think of those lines of old Goethe —Schade, dass die Natur nur einen Mensch aus dir schuf, denn zum würdigen Mann war und zum Schelmen der Stoff."

Scion — a descendent. Reginald Musgrave, for example, is said to be a descendent of a very old British family in *The Adventure of the Musgrave Ritual*. "He was indeed a scion of one of the very oldest families in the kingdom, though his branch was a cadet one which had separated from the northern Musgraves some time in the sixteenth century."

Scorbutic — a person who looks to be affected by scurvy, the vitamin C deficiency which causes bleeding gums and open sores. This is how Watson describes Shinwell Johnson, who is investigating for Holmes in the more unsavoury parts of London, in *The Adventure of the Illustrious Client*. "We found him sure enough, a huge, coarse, red-faced, scorbutic man, with a pair of vivid black eyes which were the only external sign of the very cunning mind within."

Scourge — a kind of lash or whip used either for punishing or during sessions of torture. This is what Holmes first thinks has caused the injuries on the back of poor Fitzory McPherson in *The Adventure of The Lion's Mane*. "Some human hand was on the handle of that scourge, if indeed it was a scourge which inflicted the injuries. His circle of acquaintances in this lonely place was surely limited."

Scurvy — as well as the name of the well-known disease which befell many a sailor and a pirate, scurvy is also a word which can be used to mean worthless or something which is contemptible. Mr. Thaddeus Sholto declines praise from Mary Morstan in *The Sign of Four*, when she admires his arrangement of sending her one pearl a year from his family's ill-gotten treasure. "We had plenty of money ourselves. I desired no more. Besides, it would have been such bad taste to have treated a young lady in so scurvy a fashion."

Scylla and Charybdis — two figures from Greek mythology, they are said to have been two sea monsters on either side of the Messina strait and were extremely dangerous. If a person were to sail past Scylla they would be closer to Charybdis and vice versa. The phrase itself means something which is between two evils, like between a rock and a hard place. Used by Watson at the start of *The Adventure of the Resident Patient*, on the difficulties of writing of the cases of Holmes. "The small matter which I have chronicled under the heading of *A Study in Scarlet*, and that other later one connected with the loss of the Gloria Scott, may serve as examples of this Scylla and Charybdis which are forever threatening the historian."

Secret Societies of Italy — this is the umbrella name for a group of different societies which were present in Italy in the 19th century, including the Carbonari who were mentioned in *The Adventure of the Red Circle*. It also includes the Freemasons and Young Italy. Most were reactionary and revolutionary societies, volatile in their execution of their ideology. In part two of *A Study in Scarlet*, John Ferrier lists it amongst historical religious extremist groups to highlight the scare tactics used by the Mormons to ensure devotion to the faith. "Not the Inquisition of Seville, nor the German Vehmgericht, nor the Secret Societies of Italy, were ever able to put a more formidable machinery in motion than that which cast a cloud over the State of Utah."

Sepoys — is the name given to Indian soldiers who were serving under the command of the British Army or under any other European orders up until the early 20th century. In *The Sign of Four*, Jonathan Small explains the terrible conditions in which he has suffered before trying to claim the Agra treasure from Bartholomew Sholto. "A little further up the road Dawson himself was lying on his face, quite dead, with an empty revolver in his hand and four Sepoys lying across each other in front of him."

Sepulchre — a chamber, sometimes cut in rock or built of stone, in which a dead person is laid or buried and was to be the fate of the butler Brunton in *The Adventure of the Musgrave Ritual*. "Was it a chance that the wood had slipped, and that the stone had shut Brunton into what had become his sepulchre?"

Sententiously — to talk in self-righteous or pithy sayings. In *A Study in Scarlet* it is used to convey the tone of Sherlock Holmes voice as he is lectured by Gregson on the importance of retaining and following the smallest amount of information. "'To a great mind, nothing is little,' remarked Holmes, sententiously."

Sere and yellow — another way to describe a fellow who is advancing in years and is a quote from Shakespeare's Macbeth, "Is fall'n into the sere, the yellow leaf; And that which should accompany old age." In *A Study in Scarlet*, Sherlock Holmes uses it to explain to Watson how he could arrive at an approximation of a man's age from his stride, "Well, if a man can stride four and a half feet without the smallest effort, he can't be quite in the sere and yellow."

Sheeny — a less than complimentary slang word for a person who is Jewish. In *The Adventure of the Stock Broker's Clerk*, Mr. Pycroft uses the word to describe Arthur Pinner. "In he walked, a middle-sized, dark-haired, dark-eyed, black-bearded man, with a touch of the sheeny about his nose."

Shikari — an Indian word meaning hunter or a hunting guide. In *The Adventure of the Empty House*, this is what Holmes calls Sebastian Moran as he goads him for his failure to shoot and kill him. "'I wonder that my very simple stratagem could deceive so old a shikari,' said Holmes. 'It must be very familiar to you.'"

Shoving the queer — a rather out-dated phrase now but it means the act of trying to pass and spend counterfeit money. This was one of the reasons for Jack McMurdo having to leave Chicago after the shooting of Jonas Pinto in part two of *The Valley of Fear*. As McMurdo meets an old Chicago police officer at his lodge, it is revealed that the enquiries about the convenient murder have run cold. "'Well, his death came in uncommon handy for you, or they would have had you for shoving the queer. Well, we can let that be bygones; for, between you and me.'"

Singular — something which is distinguished by its superiority, something out of the ordinary or that creates an exception. This is the word that is most familiar to lovers of Sherlock Holmes and not, as some may think, the word "elementary." There are well over a hundred uses of the phrase "singular" in the Canon and the majority of these are to emphasize and hone in on a clue or piece of evidence which may be vital to solving a case. In *Silver Blaze*, Holmes recounts the significance of one specific item in connection with the murder of John Straker. "You cannot have forgotten the singular knife which was found in the dead man's hand, a knife which certainly no sane man would choose for a weapon."

Skein — a coil or length of string which has been wrapped around a reel. The idea of problems being tangled string is a recurring theme in Holmes's deductions and in *The Adventure of the Twisted Man*, he endeavours to untangle the mystery of Professor Presbury's biting dog. "The practical application of what I have said is very close to the problem which I am investigating. It is a tangled skein, you understand, and I am looking for a loose end."

Slatternly — a woman whose appearance is untidy, scruffy or dirty. In *The Adventure of the Golden Pince-Nez*, Holmes explains his deductions about the owner of the delicate pince-nez to the astonishment of Watson and Hopkins. "As to her being a person of remitment and well dressed, they are, as you perceive, handsomely mounted in solid gold, and it is inconceivable that anyone who wore such glasses could be slatternly in other respects."

Slop-shop — one of my favourite words found within the Holmes stories. This is a shop where a person would buy cheap, ready-made clothes. Near one of these stores is located the Bar of Gold opium den, the location of a missing Mr. Isa Whitney in *The Man with the Twisted Lip*. "Between a slop-shop and a gin-shop, approached by a steep flight of steps leading down to a black gap like the mouth of a cave, I found the den of which I was in search."

Slow-worm — a creature that is neither a worm nor, despite its looks, a snake. It is actually a legless lizard, smooth and normally brown or copper-coloured. In *The Sign* *of Four*, Watson makes his way through the house of Mr. Sherman, dodging badgers, biting stoats and a slow-worm in order to get to Toby the dog. "'Don't mind that, sir: it's only a slow-worm. It hain't got no fangs, so I gives it the run o' the room, for it keeps the beetles down.'"

Smoking concerts — these were live music concerts for audiences consisting only of men. It was a chance for them to hear new music, smoke and talk about political matters in the absence of women. Watson makes reference to them in *The Valley of Fear*, as he describes John Douglas and how he integrated himself into the county society of Sussex. "...he soon acquired a great popularity among the villagers, subscribing handsomely to all local objects, and attending their smoking concerts and other functions, where, having a remarkably rich tenor voice, he was always ready to oblige with an excellent song."

Solatium — a type of compensation or something given as a consolation. Holmes warns Watson of Moriarty's reputation and describes his guarded and litigious personality which would take to court any person who would libel him as a criminal in *The Valley of Fear*. "But so aloof is he from general suspicion, so immune from criticism, so admirable in his management and self-effacement, that for those very words that you have uttered he could hale you to a court and emerge with your year's pension as a solatium for his wounded character."

Solicitude — being in a state of concern or anxiety over something or someone. In *The Adventure of the Mazarin Stone*, Billy the house boy shows some concern that Holmes is working much too hard. "Billy glanced with some solicitude at the closed door of the bedroom. 'I think he's in bed and asleep,' he said."

Sonomy — also written as Isonomy in the British publication. It refers to the horse, Isonomy who was an actual, and rather famous, thoroughbred racehorse and sire. This reference added a touch of realism to the story of missing Wessex Cup favourite in *Silver Blaze*. "'Silver Blaze,' said he, 'is from the Isonomy stock, and holds as brilliant a record as his famous ancestor.'"

Sonorous — imposingly deep and full. In *A Study in Scarlet*, it is used to describe Holmes's violin playing in regards to his moods. At times demonstrating his playful and musical personality to laying the violin on his lap and noisily plucking at the instrument at times of ennui. "Sometimes the chords were sonorous and melancholy. Occasionally they were fantastic and cheerful. Clearly they reflected the thoughts which possessed him."

Sottish — When a person's behaviour is stupid and idiotic as a consequence of taking a substance, usually drink. In the case of *The Man with the Twisted Lip*, it is opium and how Holmes describes the state of poor, confused, Isa Whitney. "If you would have the great kindness to get rid of that sottish friend of yours I should be exceedingly glad to have a little talk with you."

Speciously — something which seems to be right or true but is actually false. Said by Holmes, to Watson as they discuss the case of *The Man with the Twisted Lip*, in a carriage ride to Lee, near Kent. "No, sir, but the facts might be met speciously enough."

St. Vitus's Dance — a disease of the nervous system brought on, usually, after a streptococcal infection from childhood. It's called St. Vitus's Dance due to the involuntary movements of the face, hands and feet and is suffered by Mr. Farquhar in *The Adventure of the Stock Broker's Clerk*. "Old Mr. Farquhar, from whom I purchased it, had at one time an excellent general practice; but his age, and an affliction of the nature of St. Vitus's Dance from which he suffered, had very much thinned it."

Stormy petrel — a person who enjoys conflict or attracts and delights in controversy. Holmes exclaims to Colonel Hayter in *The Adventure of the Reigate Squire* that he probably regrets having him to visit after the murderous adventure he has taken them on. "I am afraid, my dear Colonel, that you must regret the hour that you took in such a stormy petrel as I am." It can also be found in *The Naval Treaty*, where Holmes famously, says, "You are the stormy petrel of crime, Watson."

Subcutaneously — something which is done just under the skin, usually associated with an injection but, in this case, it is how John Straker aimed to nick the tendon and make lame the eponymous horse in *Silver Blaze*. "...it is possible to make a slight nick upon the tendons of a horse's ham, and to do it subcutaneously, so as to leave absolutely no trace."

Sucking Dove — Taken from Shakespeare's *A Midsummer Night's Dream* and spoken by the character Bottom, "But I will aggravate my voice so that I will roar you as gently as any sucking dove. I will roar you an 'twere any nightingale." In *His Last Bow*, it is used by Von Bork and Baron Von Herling as they talk of the traitor Altamont, "Besides he is not a traitor. I assure you that our most pan Germanic Junker is a sucking dove in his feelings towards England as compared with a real bitter Irish-American."

Supposititious — a fraudulent substitution or a fake being swapped for the real thing. As Holmes and Watson try to untangle the murder of Mr. Douglas in *The Valley of Fear*, Holmes comes to the conclusion that Barker and Mrs. Douglas are lying to cover something up, but what? "Well, now, to continue our supposititious case, the couple — not necessarily a guilty couple — realize after the murderer is gone that they have placed themselves in a position in which it may be difficult for them to prove that they did not themselves either do the deed or connive at it."

Supraorbital — this is part of the forehead, referring to the area above the eye sockets and the location of the eyebrows. In *The Hound of the Baskervilles*, Dr James Mortimer, who has returned as a client as well as to retrieve his walking stick, is fascinated with the facial features of Holmes. "You interest me very much, Mr. Holmes. I had hardly expected so dolichocephalic a skull or such well-marked supraorbital development."

Surds — relating to mathematics and is a quantity which cannot be expressed using rational numbers. In *The Adventure of the Lion's Mane*, it is how Holmes describes the life comforts of math teacher Ian Murdoch. "He seemed to live in some high, abstract region of surds and conic sections, with little to connect him with ordinary life."

Surfeit — to have something in an excessive amount as, in *The Problem of Thor Bridge*, where Watson says that some cases have been kept back from the readers to stop them from becoming fed up with Sherlock Holmes. "There remain a considerable residue of cases of greater or less interest which I might have edited before had I not feared to give the public a surfeit which might react upon the reputation of the man whom above all others I revere."

Tang-yin — was a Chinese scholar, painter and poet and is considered one of the Four Masters of the Ming Dynasty. His writings were one of the things learned, in just 24 hours, by Watson in *The Adventure of the Illustrious Client* when Holmes asked him to familiarise himself with all forms of Chinese pottery. "...the marks of the Hung-wu and the beauties of the Yung-lo, the writings of Tang-ying, and the glories of the primitive period of the Sung and the Yuan. I was charged with all this information when I called upon Holmes next evening."

Tantalus — a type of stand or cabinet where drink decanters are locked whilst still being visible. In *The Adventure of Black Peter*, Stanley Hopkins recounts seeing one as he describes the murder scene to Holmes and Watson. "Yes; there was a tantalus containing brandy and whisky on the sea-chest. It is of no importance to us, however, since the decanters were full, and it had therefore not been used."

Tenable — something which can be defended against an attack. Holmes lays out the theory of Mr. Alexander Holder's assertion that his son has tried to steal from him to make obvious the inconsistencies in *The Adventure of the Beryl Coronet*. "You suppose that your son came down from his bed, went, at great risk, to your dressing-room, opened your bureau, took out your coronet, broke off by main force a small portion of it, went off to some other place, concealed three gems out of the thirty-nine, with such skill that nobody can find them, and then returned with the other thirty-six into the room in which he exposed himself to the greatest danger of being discovered. I ask you now, is such a theory tenable?"

Tête-à-tête — a meeting or a conversation between two people, translated from the French meaning head to head. In part one of *The Adventure of Wisteria Lodge*, it is how Mr. Scott Eccles describes his visit to the lodge. "The whole place was depressing. Our dinner was tête-à-tête, and though my host did his best to be entertaining, his thoughts seemed to continually wander, and he talked so vaguely and wildly that I could hardly understand him."

The game is not worth the candle — a phrase which, some say, goes as far back as the late 1500s - early 1600s and refers to an activity at night which would need to be done by candlelight. Candles were, at that time, an expense and so if the activity were unproductive or unyielding it was a waste of a candle and, as such, a waste of money. It was also used in gambling circles at that time. If you were to play cards for money at night and lose, then the game was not worth the price of the candle. In *The Sign of Four*, Watson uses the phrase in an attempt to deter Holmes from his drug use and the permanent damage it may do to his brain. "...it is a pathological and morbid process, which involves increased tissue-change and may at last leave a permanent weakness. You know, too, what a black reaction comes upon you. Surely the game is hardly worth the candle."

The Martyrdom of Man — a book by William Winwood Reade, who was a British historian and explorer, in which he examined the exploration of the West using ideas of philosophy, liberalism and secularism. The book was thought of, by some, as an attack on Christianity but is also said to have been a favourite book of Arthur Conan Doyle. In *The Sign of Four*, Holmes offers the book to Watson as something to read as he starts his new investigation. "I have some few references to make. Let me recommend this book, one of the most remarkable ever penned. It is Winwood Reade's Martyrdom of Man. I shall be back in an hour."

Thrice is he armed who hath his quarrel just — is a quote from *Henry VI, part 2*, Act 3, Scene 2 spoken by King Henry himself, "What stronger breastplate than a heart untainted! Thrice is he armed that hath his quarrel just, And he but naked, though lock'd up in steel Whose conscience with injustice is corrupted." This is another example of Holmes quoting Shakespeare, this time in *The Disappearance of Lady Frances Carfax*, Holmes prepares to face the kidnapper of Lady Frances. "Well, well, we shall be strong enough. 'Thrice is he armed who hath his quarrel just.' We simply can't afford to wait for the police or to keep within the four corners of the law."

Thucydides — a Greek historian, most widely known for his historical analysis of the Peloponnesian War in which he fought on the Athenian side. An extract of his writing formed part of the exam paper in *The Adventure of the Three Students*. "To-day about three o'clock the proofs of this paper arrived from the printers. The exercise consists of half a chapter of Thucydides. I had to read it over carefully, as the text must be absolutely correct."

Toilet — or toileted, used frequently in the Canon and, despite what the implications may mean now, in this context it simply means the act or process of dressing or grooming which includes bathing and brushing or styling one's hair. In *The Adventure of the Three Students*, Watson exclaims, "At eight in the morning he came into my room just as I had finished my toilet."

Tokay — are wines which come from the Tokaj region in Hungary or the adjoining Slovakia, famous for their sweet wines. This is how Von Bork and Von Herling plan to celebrate their victory in *His Last Bow*. "'...you can put a triumphant finish to your record in England. What! Tokay!' He indicated a heavily sealed dust-covered bottle which stood with two high glasses upon a salver."

Tor — a bare and rocky mountain or a rough and craggy hill. During an unsettling conversation with Mr. Stapleton out on the moor in *The Hound of the Baskervilles*, Watson mentions that has been told of deadly mires and haunting noises. Mr. Stapleton says that some residents believe that the moaning sound is "The Hound" calling for its prey. A rattled Watson starts to feel uneasy in his environment. "Nothing stirred over the vast expanse save a pair of ravens, which croaked loudly from a tor behind us."

Torpor — a lethargy or mental inactivity. This is a phrase which Dr Watson uses to describe the dual moods of Sherlock Holmes in *A Study in Scarlet*, one when he is active and on a case, and the other when his mind becomes dulled by inactivity. "His eyes were sharp and piercing, save during those intervals of torpor to which I have alluded."

Tortuous — something which is full of turns and twists. In the second part of *The Valley of Fear*, it is used to describe the desolate landscape of the agricultural county of Merton where the story continues after the revelation in part one. "Above the dark and often scarcely penetrable woods upon their flanks, the high, bare crowns of the mountains, white snow, and jagged rock towered upon each flank, leaving a long, winding, tortuous valley in the centre."

Tracery — a type of ornamental work which is usually delicate and interlaced, such as a wood carving or cast-iron work. Watson describes Baskerville Hall as he drives up to the house in *The Hound of the Baskervilles*, impressed by the construction of the building and its surroundings. "A few minutes later we had reached the lodge-gates, a maze of fantastic tracery in wrought iron, with weather-bitten pillars on either side, blotched with lichens, and surmounted by the boars' heads of the Baskervilles."

Traduce — to speak ill of a person or to spread lies about him and damage his public reputation. As Holmes talks passionately about Moriarty in *The Valley of Fear*, he explains to Watson about his much-prized reputation as a mathematics genius and his standing as such. Who would dare go up against such a man and reveal his criminality? "Is this a man to traduce? Foul mouthed doctor and slandered professor — such would be your respective roles! That's genius, Watson."

Treatise — a piece of writing which is more significant and in depth than an essay. It is systematic and formal which includes investigation, methodical argument and discourse. This is something that the dour-faced Dr Leslie Armstrong mentions during his strained conversation with Holmes in *The Adventure of the Missing Three-Quarter*, "At the present moment, for example, I should be writing a treatise instead of conversing with you."

Tremulous — a sound which is quivering or shaking slightly. In *The Sign of Four*, it is Toby the dog who yelps and yowls excitedly as he starts up on the scent of the suspected murderer of Bartholomew Sholto. "The creature instantly broke into a succession of high, tremulous yelps, and, with his nose on the ground, and his tail in the air, pattered off upon the trail at a pace which strained his leash and kept us at the top of our speed."

Trip hammer — this is a large industrial piece of powered hammering equipment used in mining or agriculture and kept, usually, within a special mill house. In the conclusion of *The Valley of Fear*, Holmes explains that the death of Mr. Douglas, as he will continue to be known to him, was not carried out by blundering criminals but was the work of Moriarty. He tells Watson how Moriarty must always win, even if that means turning his great brain to the destruction of a small man "'...It is crushing the nut with the trip hammer — an absurd extravagance of energy — but the nut is very effectually crushed all the same.'"

Truculent — aggressively defiant or eager and quick to argue. Such was the mood of Holmes and Watson as they made their way to force entry into Appledore Towers in *The Adventure of Charles Augustus Milverton*. "With our black silk face-coverings, which turned us into two of the most truculent figures in London, we stole up to the silent, gloomy house."

Tumultuously — an action of excitement, disorientation or uproar. Used by John Openshaw to describe his uncle's behaviour after being sent five dried orange pips in an envelope in *The Five Orange Pips*. "When these hot fits were over, however, he would rush tumultuously in at the door and lock and bar it behind him, like a man who can brazen it out no longer against the terror which lies at the roots of his soul."

Turbid — something which is muddy or cloudy or something which also contains particles within it. Watson writes about the Manor House of Birlstone in *The Valley of Fear*, and describes the moats which encircle it. "A small stream fed it and continued beyond it, so that the sheet of water, though turbid, was never ditch-like or unhealthy."

'Tween decks — the space between two continuous decks on a ship or any deck below the main deck. In his letter to his son in *The Adventure of the Gloria Scott*, Mr. Trevor recounts his adventure and escape from the prison ship and the shame he has carried with him. "The two warders had been shot and thrown overboard, and so also had the third mate. Prendergast then descended into the 'tween-decks and with his own hands cut the throat of the unfortunate surgeon."

Ulster — the name of a man's long overcoat, usually made of rough cloth. In *A Study in Scarlet*, an ulster is worn by Watson during his part in the deception of Irene Adler. It is also the coat worn by Adler when she disguises herself as a man to bid goodnight to Holmes outside his home. "I hardened my heart, and took the smoke-rocket from under my ulster. After all, I thought, we are not injuring her."

Ululation — a sound, much like a howl, which is used to express grief or some overwhelming emotion. Holmes explains to Watson that he does not trust the reactions of Mrs. Douglas to the death of her husband in *The Valley of Fear*, and he talks of how she seems to be missing the emotional outpourings which one would expect to see from a grieving wife. "It was badly stage-managed; for even the rawest investigators must be struck by the absence of the usual feminine ululation. If there had been nothing else, this incident alone would have suggested a prearranged conspiracy to my mind."

Unheeded — Something which is heard but ignored. In *A Study in Scarlet*, Watson describes Holmes' demeanour when his mind is hot on a chase. "...his mind was so absolutely concentrated upon the matter before him that a question or remark fell unheeded upon his ears."

Un sot trouve toujours un plus sot qui l'admire — which is translated from the French as "a fool always finds a greater fool to admire him" and was written by Nicolas Boileau-Despréaux in *The Art of Poetry* in 1674. The phrase is used by Holmes *in A Study in Scarlet* after Watson finds the misguided praise of Gregson irksome. "If the man is caught, it will be on account of their exertions; if he escapes, it will be in spite of their exertions. It's heads I win and tails you lose. Whatever they do, they will have followers. 'Un sot trouve toujours un plus sot qui l'admire.'"

Uriah and Bathsheba — a biblical story. Bathsheba was the wife of Uriah but fell pregnant by King David. David planned to bring Uriah back from battle early in an attempt to force a union between Bathsheba and her husband so he might think the child was his. When this failed he placed Uriah on the front line instead where he was certain to be killed. When he died, David married Bathsheba. The story has many similarities to that which is experienced by Henry Wood in *The Adventure of the Crooked Man* and the reason, theorises Holmes, that James Barclay was called David by his wife. "David strayed a little occasionally, you know, and on one occasion in the same direction as Sergeant James Barclay. You remember the small affair of Uriah and Bathsheba?"

Valetudinarian — is a person who is always worried and highly anxious about his health. It's a more dated term for, what we may describe today, as a hypochondriac. Such is the state of the nervous Mr. Thaddeus Sholto in *The Sign of Four*. As he remarks to his guests after he puts on his many layers of clothing despite the warm evening. "'My health is somewhat fragile,' he remarked, as he led the way down the passage. 'I am compelled to be a valetudinarian.'"

Vehemence — to say something forcefully or with a great intensity of expression or feeling. Holmes reacts with humour at poor Watson's anger at his drug use in *The Sign of Four*. "He smiled at my vehemence. 'Perhaps you are right, Watson,' he said.' I suppose that its influence is physically a bad one.'"

Veldt — the name, in parts of South Africa, for the open countryside which is full of shrubs and thinly forested areas, much like the Australian bush. After sleeping outside for so long, even the drab rooms of Tuxbury Old Hall were a welcome comfort to James M. Dodd in *The Adventure of the Blanched Soldier*. "It was a large, bare room on the ground floor, as gloomy as the rest of the house, but after a year of sleeping upon the veldt, Mr. Holmes, one is not too particular about one's quarters."

Venerable — a person who is given a great deal of respect either because of his knowledge or because of his standing, but especially because of his age. In *The Hound of the Baskervilles*, Dr Mortimer explains to Holmes the people who would inherit the Baskerville fortune should something untoward happen to Sir Henry. Holmes enquires about the look and character of the next in line, Mr. James Desmond. "...he once came down to visit Sir Charles. He is a man of venerable appearance and of saintly life. I remember that he refused to accept any settlement from Sir Charles, though he pressed it upon him."

Vieni — the Italian word for "come" and flashed in code by Holmes in *The Adventure of the Red Circle* in order to trick Emilia Lucca into coming to the crime scene to explain the death of Giuseppe Gorgiano. "Your cipher was not difficult, madam. Your presence here was desirable. I knew that I had only to flash 'Vieni' and you would surely come."

View-halloa — during the act of fox hunting this is the shout made by a hunter upon seeing a fox and so alerting the riders and dogs. Used in *The Adventure of the Devil's Foot* by Watson as he describes the look on the face of Holmes as a fresh mystery comes crashing through their doors. "I glared at the intrusive vicar with no very friendly eyes; but Holmes took his pipe from his lips and sat up in his chair like an old hound who hears the view-halloa."

Vitriol — oil of vitriol is another term for sulphuric acid. It was this that was thrown at Baron Adelbert Gruner by a mysterious woman in *The Adventure of the Illustrious Client* as Sherlock Holmes made off with his infamous book. "The vitriol was eating into it everywhere and dripping from the ears and the chin. One eye was already white and glazed. The other was red and inflamed."

Voil`a tout — translated as "that is it" or "that is all" meaning the end of the whole matter. In *A Case of Identity*, Holmes cries it in an exclamation at the denouement of his case. "The same post brought me a letter from Westhouse & Marbank, of Fenchurch Street, to say that the description tallied in every respect with that of their employee, James Windibank. Voil`a tout!"

Voraciously — an eager craving for consuming large quantities of food. How Watson describes Holmes in *The Five Orange Pips* as he enthusiastically eats after, what seems to have been, a long and difficult day of detective work. "He walked up to the sideboard, and tearing a piece from the loaf he devoured it voraciously, washing it down with a long draught of water."

Vox populi, vox Dei — translated from the Latin as, "the voice of the people is the voice of God" and is spoken by Holmes as he, and Watson, give their verdict in the case of *The Adventure of the Abbey Grange*. He decrees his final judgement (with Watson as the jury) as to the moral innocence of Captain Croker. "Vox populi, vox Dei. You are acquitted, Captain Croker. So long as the law does not find some other victim you are safe from me."

Weald — an area which was previously wooded and included parts of Kent, Surrey, and East Sussex. In *The Adventure of Black Peter*, on the way to the case, Watson comments on the journey from Wayside station. "...widespread woods, which were once part of that great forest which for so long held the Saxon invaders at bay — the impenetrable "weald," for sixty years the bulwark of Britain."

Wheal — a raised and reddened area of skin, a swollen mark. In *The Man with the Twisted Lip*, it is used to describe the disfigured face of the beggar Hugh Boone. "A broad wheal from an old scar ran right across it from eye to chin, and by its contraction had turned up one side of the upper lip."

Wheat pit — a place of exchange or a market where wheat stocks are bought and sold. In *The Adventure of the Three Garridebs*, Mr. Nathan Garrideb explains to Holmes and Watson the origins of Alexander Hamilton Garrideb's fortune. "He made his money in real estate, and afterwards in the wheat pit at Chicago, but he spent it in buying up as much land as would make one of your counties,"

Whetstone — a stone for sharpening knives and other cooking utensils. In *The Adventure of the Creeping Man*, Watson describes himself as a tool which Holmes used, at times, to sharpen his mind. "I was a whetstone for his mind. I stimulated him. He liked to think aloud in my presence."

Whiskey-pegs — this is a drink made from whiskey mixed with sugar and lemon or lime juice as mentioned by Jonathan Small in *The Sign of Four*, when describing how nonchalantly his boss Mr. Abelwhite took news of the great mutiny. "He had it in his head that the affair had been exaggerated, and that it would blow over as suddenly as it had sprung up. There he sat on his veranda, drinking whiskey-pegs and smoking cheroots, while the country was in a blaze about him."

Whole-souled — another term for wholeheartedly, something which is fuelled by enthusiasm or devotion. After Watson declares that Barker and Mrs. Douglas must be guilty of the murder of Mr. Douglas, Holmes is quick to chastise him for his turn of phrase and appalling directness in *The Valley of Fear*. "If you put it that Mrs. Douglas and Barker know the truth about the murder, and are conspiring to conceal it, then I can give you a whole-souled answer. I am sure they do. But your more deadly proposition is not so clear."

Wide-awake — a hat made of soft felt which has a wide brim and a low crown. This is the hat held by the client Mr. Grant Munro as he first enters Baker Street in *The Adventure* *of the Yellow Face.* "He was well but quietly dressed in a dark-grey suit, and carried a brown wide-awake in his hand."

Winwood Reade — Winwood Reade was a British historian, explorer, and philosopher who wrote, widely, about secularism. His book *The Martyrdom of Man* (a favourite book of Arthur Conan Doyle) was referenced earlier in *The Sign of Four*, as a book Watson should read. Later in the story Holmes references him again to Watson and Jones as they watch the men in the shipyards. "'Winwood Reade is good upon the subject,' said Holmes. 'He remarks that, while the individual man is an insoluble puzzle, in the aggregate he becomes a mathematical certainty. You can, for example, never foretell what any one man will do, but you can say with precision what an average number will be up to."

Wiper — when, in *The Sign of Four*, Mr. Sherman threatens Watson with a wiper, he is actually talking about a viper snake. It was an interesting habit of Cockneys in the 1800s to swap the v and the w sounds, although by the start of the 1900s this had, pretty much, stopped altogether. "'Go on!' yelled the voice. 'So help me gracious, I have a wiper in the bag, an' I'll drop it on your 'ead if you don't hook it."

Wir sind gewohnt, daß die Menschen verhöhnen was sie nicht verstehen — which translates from the German as "we are used to seeing that Man despises what he never comprehends" and is a quote from Johann Wolfgang von Goethe's *Faust*. Holmes quotes this to Watson after explaining the instructions they must both follow in order to close in on the killer of Bartholomew Sholto in *The Sign of Four*. Watson is to collect Toby the dog and Holmes is to interview the staff at Pondicherry Lodge before patiently listening to Athelney Jones' methods of 'solving' the case. "Then I shall study the great Jones's methods and listen to his not too delicate sarcasms. 'Wir sind gewohnt, daß die Menschen verhöhnen was sie nicht verstehen.' Goethe is always pithy.'"

Zeppelin — a rigid, motor driven airship which was pioneered by Count Ferdinand von Zeppelin at the start of the 1900s. These airships were used by the Germans in the "strategic bombing campaign" against Britain during World War I. There were more than fifty "Zeppelin raids" over the UK during the war and this is, chillingly, referred to by Baron Von Herling in *His Last Bow*. "The heavens, too, may not be quite so peaceful if all that the good Zeppelin promises us comes true."

Also from MX Publishing

MX Publishing is the world's largest specialist Sherlock Holmes publisher, with over a hundred titles and fifty authors creating the latest in Sherlock Holmes fiction and non-fiction.

From traditional short stories and novels to travel guides and quiz books, MX Publishing cater for all Holmes fans.

The collection includes leading titles such as *Benedict Cumberbatch In Transition* and *The Norwood Author* which won the 2011 Howlett Award (Sherlock Holmes Book of the Year).

MX Publishing also has one of the largest communities of Holmes fans on Facebook with regular contributions from dozens of authors.

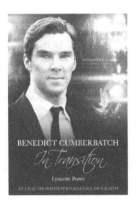

www.mxpublishing.com

Also from MX Publishing

  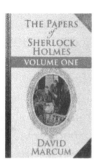

Our bestselling books are our short story collections;

'Lost Stories of Sherlock Holmes' , 'The Outstanding Mysteries of Sherlock Holmes', The Papers of Sherlock Holmes Volume 1 and 2, 'Untold Adventures of Sherlock Holmes' (and the sequel 'Studies in Legacy) and 'Sherlock Holmes in Pursuit', 'The Cotswold Werewolf and Other Stories of Sherlock Holmes' – and many more……

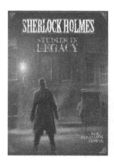  

www.mxpublishing.com

Also from MX Publishing

"Phil Growick's, 'The Secret Journal of Dr Watson', is an adventure which takes place in the latter part of Holmes and Watson's lives. They are entrusted by HM Government (although not officially) and the King no less to undertake a rescue mission to save the Romanovs, Russia's Royal family from a grisly end at the hand of the Bolsheviks. There is a wealth of detail in the story but not so much as would detract us from the enjoyment of the story. Espionage, counter-espionage, the ace of spies himself, double-agents, double-crossers...all these flit across the pages in a realistic and exciting way. All the characters are extremely well-drawn and Mr. Growick, most importantly, does not falter with a very good ear for Holmesian dialogue indeed. Highly recommended. A five-star effort."
The Baker Street Society

www.mxpublishing.com

Also from MX Publishing

The Missing Authors Series

Sherlock Holmes and The Adventure of The Grinning Cat
Sherlock Holmes and The Nautilus Adventure
Sherlock Holmes and The Round Table Adventure

"Joseph Svec, III is brilliant in entwining two endearing and enduring classics of literature, blending the factual with the fantastical; the playful with the pensive; and the mischievous with the mysterious. We shall, all of us young and old, benefit with a cup of tea, a tranquil afternoon, and a copy of Sherlock Holmes, The Adventure of the Grinning Cat."

Amador County Holmes Hounds Sherlockian Society

www.mxpublishing.com

Also from MX Publishing

The American Literati Series

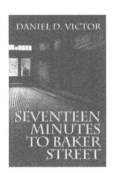

The Final Page of Baker Street
The Baron of Brede Place
Seventeen Minutes To Baker Street

"The really amazing thing about this book is the author's ability to call up the 'essence' of both the Baker Street 'digs' of Holmes and Watson as well as that of the 'mean streets' of Marlowe's Los Angeles. Although none of the action takes place in either place, Holmes and Watson share a sense of camaraderie and self-confidence in facing threats and problems that also pervades many of the later tales in the Canon. Following their conversations and banter is a return to Edwardian England and its certainties and hope for the future. This is definitely the world before The Great War."
Philip K Jones

www.mxpublishing.com

Also from MX Publishing

The Detective and The Woman Series

The Detective and The Woman
The Detective, The Woman and The Winking Tree
The Detective, The Woman and The Silent Hive

"The book is entertaining, puzzling and a lot of fun. I believe the author has hit on the only type of long-term relationship possible for Sherlock Holmes and Irene Adler. The details of the narrative only add force to the romantic defects we expect in both of them and their growth and development are truly marvelous to watch. This is not a love story. Instead, it is a coming-of-age tale starring two of our favorite characters."
Philip K Jones

www.mxpublishing.com

Also from MX Publishing

The Sherlock Holmes and Enoch Hale Series

The Amateur Executioner
The Poisoned Penman
The Egyptian Curse

"The Amateur Executioner: Enoch Hale Meets Sherlock Holmes", the first collaboration between Dan Andriacco and Kieran McMullen, concerns the possibility of a Fenian attack in London. Hale, a native Bostonian, is a reporter for London's Central News Syndicate - where, in 1920, Horace Harker is still a familiar figure, though far from revered. "The Amateur Executioner" takes us into an ambiguous and murky world where right and wrong aren't always distinguishable. I look forward to reading more about Enoch Hale."
Sherlock Holmes Society of London

www.mxpublishing.com

179

Also from MX Publishing

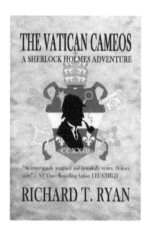

When the papal apartments are burgled in 1901, Sherlock Holmes is summoned to Rome by Pope Leo XII. After learning from the pontiff that several priceless cameos that could prove compromising to the church, and perhaps determine the future of the newly unified Italy, have been stolen, Holmes is asked to recover them. In a parallel story, Michelangelo, the toast of Rome in 1501 after the unveiling of his Pieta, is commissioned by Pope Alexander VI, the last of the Borgia pontiffs, with creating the cameos that will bedevil Holmes and the papacy four centuries later. For fans of Conan Doyle's immortal detective, the game is always afoot. However, the great detective has never encountered an adversary quite like the one with whom he crosses swords in "The Vatican Cameos."

"An extravagantly imagined and beautifully written Holmes story"
(**Lee Child**, NY Times Bestselling author, Jack Reacher series)

Also from MX Publishing

The Conan Doyle Notes (The Hunt For Jack The Ripper) "Holmesians have long speculated on the fact that the Ripper murders aren't mentioned in the canon, though the obvious reason is undoubtedly the correct one: even if Conan Doyle had suspected the killer's identity he'd never have considered mentioning it in the context of a fictional entertainment. Ms Madsen's novel equates his silence with that of the dog in the night-time, assuming that Conan Doyle did know who the Ripper was but chose not to say – which, of course, implies that good old stand-by, the government cover-up. It seems unlikely to me that the Ripper was anyone famous or distinguished, but fiction is not fact, and "The Conan Doyle Notes" is a gripping tale, with an intelligent, courageous and very likable protagonist in DD McGil."
The Sherlock Holmes Society of London

www.mxpublishing.com

Lightning Source UK Ltd.
Milton Keynes UK
UKHW041412021119
352731UK00006BA/465/P

9 781787 053168